P. C. Doherty was born in Middlesbrough and educated at Woodcote Hall. He studied History at Liverpool and Oxford Universities and obtained a doctorate at Oxford for his thesis on Edward II and Queen Isabella. He is now the Headmaster of a school in North-East London.

He lives with his American wife and family near Epping Forest, along with a horse, cat and other sundry animals.

Also by P. C. Doherty

Satan in St Mary's
Crown in Darkness
Spy in Chancery

The Angel of Death

P. C. Doherty

First published in Great Britain in 1989
by Robert Hale Limited

First published in paperback in 1991
by HEADLINE BOOK PUBLISHING PLC

10 9 8 7 6 5 4 3 2 1

ISBN 0 7472 3694 1

Printed and bound in Great Britain by
Collins Manufacturing, Glasgow

HEADLINE BOOK PUBLISHING PLC
Headline House
79 Great Titchfield Street
London W1P 7FN

To my fellow detective and cousin,
Dominic Jones

1

O day of wrath, o day of mourning! A common feeling amongst men as the end of the century approached. They talked and gossiped about how, in the year 1299, something terrible would happen to mark the changing of the century. Men pointed to the inclement weather, the failure of crops and the outbreak of war as signs on the dark-edge of the world that the Anti-christ had been born. In the cities and villages Satan and all his imperial army had been seen singing their diabolical matins in the wet dank woods. Men believed Satan walked. His time had come and no more so than in Scotland, where King Edward I of England had led a huge army of foot and horse to bring his rebellious subjects to their knees.

If the devil did walk and if he did lurk in the darkness then surely he must have taken up his throne in the dark, wooded slopes overlooking the English camp outside Berwick. There, wrapped in a brown woollen cloak, seated on a trunk in his purple silk war pavilion, Edward of England was bitterly regretting the evil he had done that day. He poured himself a large brimming cup of blood-red Gascon wine, and sipping it while he half listened to the sounds of his camp, the calls of guards, the faint neigh of horses, the crunch of mailed feet on the crushed bracken. He was cold. A wind had swept in from the grey, cruel North Sea and, despite all his attempts to keep warm, Edward of England shivered. He wanted to go down on his knees and confess to his creator his terrible sin. Cain's sin, the sin of anger, of murder; and yet he meant well. He had spent twenty-four years of his reign attempting to bring order to these islands, crushing the Irish, bringing the Welsh to heel and, at last, conquering the Scots. Had he not intervened and given them a king, their own noble, John Balliol? Yet what had happened? Edward felt like squeezing the cup in his hands. Balliol, conspiring with his enemies abroad, Philip of France and the King of Norway, had risen in rebellion. Edward, swearing terrible oaths, had taken his huge force north and crossed the border, sacking the priory of Coldstream and everything else in his way until he came to Berwick. He hated that town on the Scottish eastern march, full of fat burgesses who looked after their own concerns, revelling in its nickname of the Alexandria of the West.

Its citizens had seen Edward's fleet at sea and the huge force of English, Welsh and Irish: the lines of bowmen, the serried ranks of men-at-arms, the colour and panoply of his cavalry. Yet those same burgesses of Berwick had refused him entry, saying that their fealty was to John Balliol, the rebellious king. Edward had immediately ordered an all-out assault, screaming in rage when he heard how his fleet had been driven back and his soldiers were dying in their hundreds in the ditches under the walls of this rebellious city. Finally, his own nephew had received his death wound, a huge quarrel from a crossbow smashing into his unprotected face and turning it into a screaming bloody pulp. That had been the last straw for Edward. He had mounted his great warhorse Bayard and personally led the charge across the narrow ditch of Berwick and stormed the gate. In the face of such fury the Scots had given way. Once the English had seized the gates, the terrible slaughter had begun. Edward, furious with the rebellious citizens, ordered his soldiers to show no quarter and the day had been given over to sacking the city. Men, women and children were cut down in their hundreds; the wells choked with corpses; the bodies littered the streets like leaves on a windy autumn day. Churches had been sacked and horses stabled there, precious ornaments looted, silken hangings torn down. Children had not been spared; they were knifed, beheaded and impaled on lances. Women in their hundreds were raped before their throats were cut, and then the entire city was put to the torch. Edward had seen it all. A terrible descent into hell as he rode his great, black warhorse along the terror-filled, narrow streets. Eventually, he had seen one of his Irish footmen cut the throat of a woman begging for mercy and Edward had dismounted, muttering, 'Oh no! I did not wish this!' On his knees he had tried to beg God's forgiveness but God had moved away from Edward of England. The king felt it would be useless giving orders for the killing to stop now, for the English had simply run out of people to slay.

Only one place held out: the Red House owned by Fleming merchants, their own trade hall in Berwick given on the sole condition that they would always defend it against the English. The Flemings proved their loyalty, barring doors and windows; they had kept the English army at bay while they fought from room to room, even hiding in the cellars, trapping the archers Edward's captains sent down after them. The slaughter had been terrible. The house was well named, Edward mused, for by the time his attack had been beaten off there were pools of blood at the foot of its walls and huge red gashes where the blood poured down from the bodies lolling out of the windows. Tired and weary at such resistance, Edward had called off the attack and ordered the place to be burnt to the ground, closing his ears to the dreadful screams of burning men. He had sat on his horse, encased completely in black armour, a gold circlet around his helmet, watching impassively whilst the Red House burnt, ignoring the cries of the Flemings and the stench of their burning bodies.

Now it was all over. Berwick was a sea of ashes. The rebellious John Balliol had already sent messages to the king's camp, promising to do fealty, abdicate his royal rights and leave Scotland for ever. Edward was satisfied. His rule had been accepted and the rebels smashed. Treason, once again, had earned its just deserts, but Edward knew there was something wrong. Such killing, such murder, such hatred would cause new troubles to fester in Scotland, and Edward was tired. Twenty-four years a king, the sweet taste of victories, of triumphant glory, had already turned into a bitter bile. He had buried his young children in their little coffins at Westminster and St Paul's. He had also lost his adoring wife Eleanor and Robert Burnell, his faithful chancellor; all gone into the darkness. Only Edward, God's anointed, was left on this earth, attempting to bring order out of chaos.

Edward chewed nervously at a fingernail. And behind him what was happening? His usual cordial relationship with the great barons of England was also turning sour. They were beginning to object to his war taxes and arduous campaigns. They did not share his vision, so objected in an ever rising chorus of protest. Edward took a large mouthful of wine and swirled it around in his mouth, hoping it would calm the raging abscess in one of his teeth. 'All things break down,' he murmured. His rule, his health. Would he continue to spend the rest of his life in cold tents outside desolate towns? Would that be his reward for eternity? Sitting in some icy part of hell, unable to achieve what he so desired? Edward felt Satan was close. The king licked his lips. He would go south. He would rebuild Berwick and restore the priory at Coldstream. He would have masses said in all the churches, abbeys and cathedrals. He would do penance. He would talk to God. Surely a fellow monarch would understand? Edward of England cowered deeper in his cloak and listened to the wind rise outside. Was it the wind or the hymn of Satan's army camped about him, waiting for his soul? The king put the wine down and, going over to his trestle bed, lay down, praying for sleep to calm the pain in his body and soothe the iron-hard anxieties in his soul.

* * *

A few weeks later, in a small white-washed room in London, Edward might have met a man who fully understood the iron bitterness of hatred and the unquenchable hunger for vengeance. The man sat on a small stool, shrouded in his robe, the cowl pulled over his head to hide his face. He just stared at the simple altar; only the crucifix hanging above it was clear in a pool of light thrown by a solitary candle. Like Edward, the man was cold, not just because it was winter or the lack of fire in the room, but rather from an iciness which came from the innermost part of his being: a malicious hatred which dominated his every waking moment, his every thought, no matter how calm his outward appearance seemed. For this man hated the English king. A hatred which had grown like some rare exotic plant, tended carefully, nurtured every hour of the day since the news had come from Berwick. The man wanted revenge. He knew from the Bible about vengeance being the Lord's but such thoughts were no comfort. At first he had wanted vengeance for justice's sake but, now, he feasted on his hatred for the English king as he would on a good meal or savour a rich wine.

The man stirred and looked into the pool of light. Edward had achieved a great deal in Scotland and the people may well have accepted him, but there was no excuse for Berwick. The man smiled mirthlessly and once more called up the bitterness behind his revenge. 'Oh God! How could God allow it? How could he?' He thought of his younger brother, the bland face and blond hair, the simple cornflower blue eyes. How much he had trusted him! How his brother had adored him. How he had accepted, childlike, his assurances that service with Edward of England would bring him great profit. How he could move and prosper, and how no finer place existed for business and commerce than the great town and castle of Berwick.

His brother had accepted his assurances and gone, only to perish with the rest in the terrible slaughter there.

The news had come slowly through pedlars, tinkers and the odd merchant. At first, the man had refused to accept what he heard; surely no king could do that? Edward of England, who styled himself as the great saviour of the West, could never order a town with all its men, women and children to be put to the sword? Such things were now past. They were against the laws and usages of war and Edward of England reverenced the law as he did the Blessed Sacrament. But when the truth came it was even more dreadful. Yes, Edward had ordered all the citizens of Berwick to be butchered. Thousands had died; some put it as high as ten thousand, others twice that number. The town had been completely sacked, inhabitants butchered without distinction of age sex or condition. Even those who had fled to the churches were slain within sanctuary, the sacred places treated blasphemously by the ordinary English soldier. And his brother? The man closed his eyes to hide the tears. Matthew must have died, his blue eyes glazing over, their look of puzzlement hidden by death. And Matthew's wife, the little children? How many had there been? Three or four. He remembered them from two years ago, when Matthew had been in London: they were peas out of a pod with their round cherubic faces and thick masses of blond hair. They had played in the cathedral forecourt, screeching with laughter at the sheer enjoyment of life. Now their lives were gone, snuffed out like the faltering flame of a candlewick, all because of the wrath of the King of England.

The man looked at the crucifix, his lips curled back like those of a snarling dog. He recalled a line from the Bible. What was it? 'I have made a pact with the dead,' he murmured, 'with Hell. I have come to an understanding.' How could he look at that crucifix? If God had stopped talking to him, he would stop talking to God. He rose, walked over to the altar and, grabbing the crucifix, twisted it till the alabaster head hung down to the floor. He returned, sat down and looked at the blasphemy he had committed. He did not care. He got up once again and, licking his fingers, snuffed out the candle. Now he was in the dark. What he planned was indeed best planned in the dark, though, when it happened, all would see. He would call on the forces of darkness, on his own strength, guile and cunning, to bring Edward of England as low as Hell itself.

2

'*Sanctus, sanctus, sanctus.*' The priest's hymn of praise to a thrice-holy God was taken up by the choir, their singing welling up to fill the huge nave of St Paul's Cathedral. Beneath its canopy of carved stone and wood, Walter de Montfort, Dean of St Paul's, with other canons of the cathedral began the incantation which marked the beginning of the important part of this solemn High Mass. The celebrant's gold and gem-encrusted vestments dazzled the eye, their colour and light being magnified by the hundreds of beeswax candles which stood upon and around the huge, high altar. The damask white altar-cloth with its gold fringes and purple tassels was already covered in pools of pure wax. The incense rose in huge fragrant clouds, warming the cold air and doing something to hide the stench of the populace packed in the cathedral. On the right side of the sanctuary sat Edward of England in his robes of state, a silver chaplet on his steel-grey hair. His face modelled itself in a look of piety as, under heavy-lidded eyes, he watched his opponent the dean celebrate the mass of peace before that same dean launched into a lengthy sermon on whether the Church should pay its taxes.

On either side of Edward sat his temporal and spiritual lords of England. On his immediate right was Robert Winchelsea, Archbishop of Canterbury, the principal mover behind this morning's pageant, a defender of the Church's right to grow wealthy but pay nothing. Edward disliked the man, a born conniver, who hid his political ambitions behind the intricacies of Canon Law, scriptural quotations and, if these failed, appeals to Rome. Edward should have drawn comfort from his great barons but these too he did not trust. The burly Bigod, Earl of Norfolk and Marshal of his armies: Edward had once respected the man but now, looking sideways, he glimpsed Bigod's puffy, pig-like features, a man, Edward thought, prepared to go to war and fight his enemies as long as it brought great profits to his own coffers. Beside him sat Bohun, Earl of Hereford, a thin weasel-like man with a loud voice and a brain which Edward privately considered no bigger than a bead. He would go where Norfolk led.

The only men Edward did trust were behind him, the clever clerks and lawyers who aided and assisted him in his government of the country. The chief of these, Edward's Senior Clerk of the Chancery and Keeper of the Secret Seal, Hugh Corbett, stirred restlessly on the gouged wooden stool he had been given to squat upon throughout this long and lengthy service. Corbett felt guilty. He loved the mass but hated these solemn occasions when Christ and his saints were hidden by the panoply and rituals of the church. Corbett stretched his legs and looked around. Beside him, his servant Ranulf wiped his snotty nose on his sleeve and, for almost the hundredth time since the service began, attempted to clear his throat of phlegm. Corbett glared at him. He knew Ranulf was ill with a slight fever, but he also suspected his servant took great glee in reminding Corbett of how ill he actually was.

The clerk, looking round the huge, muscular frame of his king, stared up across the sanctuary. The altar was a pool of light; priests, bishops, abbots, – the lay servers of the cathedral, the whole retinue of this marvellous edifice, all in attendance now concentrated on celebrating High Mass. The choir's paean of praise eventually ended and the reedy, strident voice of Walter de Montfort began the solemn, long prayer of the Consecration. Corbett curbed his impatience. He knew the service was only a charade; once it was finished the real politics would begin. Edward of England needed money; he wanted treasure to fight Philip of France abroad and crush the rebels in Scotland. He had taxed his people and his merchants; sold privileges and concessions in order to fill his war chests but now it was the turn of the Church.

To assist him, Edward had gathered his parliament, or virtually all of it, into one sweaty mass in this cathedral. They would hear mass, make reparation with God, take the sacrament and give each other the kiss of peace. Then the real business would begin. Corbett shifted uneasily on the rough wooden stool and pulled his cloak more firmly round him. It was bitterly cold; January 1299 would, he thought, be remembered by many for the terrible snowstorms which had swept the country. Outside, the snow lay two or three feet deep, whipped up by a savage cold wind which now pierced the cracks in the cathedral doors and whistled along the nave, making the candle-light dance and everyone shiver. Corbett felt guilty for thinking such secular thoughts as the mass swept towards the solemn point of consecration when the celebrant would take the bread and wine and utter the sacred words, transforming them into Christ's body and blood. Corbett quietly struck his breast and murmured '*Miserere, Miserere!*' Beside him Ranulf sniffed once again, wiped a runny nose on his jerkin sleeve and looked sideways at Corbett, hoping his master would take note of the fresh insult. Ranulf loved Corbett but would never admit it, relishing every opportunity to stir, excite or alarm this usually serious-minded, rather grave clerk.

Corbett's mind, however, had wandered off, concentrating on the king's major problem: Edward was bankrupt. Two years ago he had debased his coinage, then he had begun to raise taxes in one parliament after another and collectors of the tax on land were sent into the shires and boroughs to claim the king's due. The demand for money was relentless: Edward was at war with France, attempting to save the English Duchy of Aquitaine from Philip IV's acquisitive clutches. Moreover, the King had recently put down a serious revolt in South Wales and only a year ago he had sacked Berwick and brought Balliol and others to their knees. Yet the rebellion in Scotland refused to subside. News had come south of a new Scottish war leader, a commoner, William the Wallace, who had fanned the flames of unrest by perpetrating secret night raids on isolated garrisons and columns, not missing any opportunity to harass and attack the English occupiers.

The wars demanded good silver. Edward had taken loans from the Italian bankers, the Frescobaldi, but now they would give no more and so he had turned on the Church. The Church was wealthy, a fat milk cow, and Edward dearly wanted to separate some of its riches from it. He had seized the tax levied by the former pope, Nicholas IV, who had nurtured grand ideas of uniting all Christendom in a new offensive against the Turk. Edward had enthusiastically taken up the idea of a crusade but had seized the money raised. He then turned to the alien priories, those houses owned by religious orders abroad, seizing their revenue and temporalities. Corbett had played a significant role in the appropriation of this ecclesiastical wealth, going through memoranda rolls, documents and charters, searching out what the king's rights were in these matters. Time and again, Corbett with barons of the exchequer and other treasury officials, had met to study long lists of rents, dues and fee-farms owing to the king. The results had been meagre, certainly not enough to finance Edward's wars abroad, so the king had begun to cast envious eyes on the wealth of the rest of the English Church. In this he met two staunch opponents: Boniface VIII in Avignon, who was totally determined on the churches in Western Christendom resuming their regular payments to the coffers of St Peter, and Robert Winchelsea, consecrated archbishop four years earlier, who had a very clear idea about his own rights and those of the English Church.

Edward had summoned both the Archbishops of Canterbury and York to meet their clergy in convocation to raise taxes. However, shortly after the sack of Berwick, matters had been complicated by Boniface VIII issuing his bull, '*Clericis Laicos*,' which Winchelsea had used to insist that the king could only tax the Church with the Church's permission. Edward, hiding his terrible anger, had bitterly agreed. Matters were further worsened, Corbett thought, as he looked along the row of dignitaries in front of him, by plotters like Bigod and Bohun, who not only resented royal taxation but also Edward's demands to accompany him abroad to fight the French. Soon these diverse plotting groups would unite and form the same opposition Edward's father and grandfather had faced when trying to raise money for disastrous wars abroad.

Corbett stared through the haze of incense at the tall emaciated figure of the chief celebrant, Walter de Montfort: Archbishop Winchelsea had decided that the Church's case – requiring its full approval before it was taxed should be put to the king by no less a person than the Dean of St Paul's, Walter de Montfort. The archbishop's choice was a quiet, deadly insult to Edward, for the dean was a member, albeit tenuously, of the great de Montfort family who forty years ago had opposed Edward and his father, King Henry. Simon de Montfort, Earl of Leicester, one of the great barons of the time, had risen in revolt, seized the government and virtually dictated his own terms to the defeated monarch, Henry III.

Edward, then Prince of Wales, had quietly accepted such demands until he had gathered sufficient forces for a counter-attack. The ensuing civil war was a bloody, vicious affair, ending only when de Montfort was killed, hacked to pieces at the Battle of Evesham. After that the de Montforts, or most of those who had survived the collapse of Earl Simon, had gone abroad, but continued a secret war against Edward, sending assassins into the country to kill him and attacking his envoys abroad. On one occasion they even murdered the king's cousin while he was at mass *en route* to Rome. Of course, Walter de Montfort was not a traitor, nor even tainted with any treason, but he was a fiery, logical, eloquent preacher and, once again, Edward would be faced by a de Montfort lecturing him on the limitations of the Crown in taxing its subjects. It would not be a pleasant meeting. Corbett had met the king just after he learnt of the choice of speaker and his anger had been uncontrollable.

'By God's mouth!' he muttered. 'Must I listen to a de Montfort tell me when and where I can get my monies from? I will not forget Winchelsea's insult. I do not bear such grudges lightly.'

Edward, when crossed, was a vindictive man, as the sack of Berwick proved. Corbett himself owed a great deal to the king. He had risen through the ranks to become a senior clerk in the chancery, with fat fees, two pleasant town houses and a manor with good land and grazing near Lewes in Sussex. Nevertheless, he was always wary of the king, for Edward's temper, since the death of his beloved Eleanor, was always fickle and his moods could swerve abruptly like a wind at sea arising suddenly to destroy anything in its path. Edward's anger could lash and vindictively punish even great lords who dared to oppose him.

Corbett suddenly reasserted himself. The consecration prayer had finished; there would be the kiss of peace before the Eucharist was shared. De Montfort, grandly attired in gold and purple copes, walked down the altar steps towards the king and, bowing, put his hands lightly on the king's shoulders and kissed him gently on each cheek.

'*Pax Domini sit semper vobiscum.*'

'*Et cum spirituo,*' the king whispered.

Then de Montfort, resplendent in liturgical robes as well

as his own arrogance, walked back to the altar where the mass continued.

The choirs sang the *Agnus Dei* emphasizing the '*miserere nobis*', their chant trailing away, lost in the high vault of the cathedral. Corbett felt himself relax; the music soothed and calmed him. There was little point in worrying and he began to search his own soul in preparation for the sacrament. The Host was elevated, the bells rung. Corbett looked at Ranulf to ensure he still had the proper pious expression. There was a short interruption in the service as the Host was passed around, the celebrant priests now in a huddle around the altar, then the chalice was circulated. Corbett saw de Montfort turn to elevate the Host to the rest of the congregation.

'*Ecce Agnus Dei, qui tollit peccata mundi*' – Behold the Lamb of God, who takes away the sins of the world. Suddenly de Montfort went rigid and the ciborium slipped from his hand, dashing the white hosts like snowflakes onto the altar steps. The man's hand went out, pointing at the king, his usually skull-like face now almost cadaverous, the skin drawn tight, the eyes bulging. Corbett rose, his hand searching for the knife beneath his cloak. De Montfort's mouth opened and shut like a landed carp, then with a loud cry he fell headlong down the steps, his skull crashing against the stone. For a few seconds there was absolute silence, followed by consternation. Several knights of the royal household ran up, pushing their way through the crowds into the sanctuary, looking around up into the nave to see if de Montfort had been brought down by some mysterious assassin. There was shouting, screaming. Corbett saw Sir Fulk Bassett, a young knight banneret and a member of Edward's household, go across the sanctuary and kneel beside de Montfort's rigid body. He gave him the most superficial look, turned and shouted across to the king.

'Sire!' Corbett saw Bassett feel the man's throat. 'I think he is dead.'

A young deacon, his gold vestments swirling around him like the dress of a woman, hurried up to Winchelsea.

'My Lord Bishop,' he stuttered, 'the priest is dead.'

Winchelsea glanced sideways at the king.

'Have his body removed,' he replied softly. 'And do not finish the service.' The man, bowing and bobbing, scurried away.

Winchelsea turned to the king. 'Your Grace,' he said wryly, 'it appears there will be no sermon.'

'And will I get my taxes, my Lord Bishop?'

'Not till this matter is resolved,' Winchelsea snapped back. He leaned over to the king. 'I must urge Your Grace to respect the rights of the Church, fought for and protected by the papacy and sealed with the blood of the martyred Becket.'

The king leaned forward, his face suffused with rage.

'Sometimes, my Lord Bishop,' he rasped quietly, 'it would appear the Blessed Becket richly deserved what he got.'

Winchelsea recoiled at such blasphemy and was about to reply when a strident, wailing cry cut across the sanctuary. Corbett, who had heard the exchange between the bishop and the king, stared around. The sound came from a slit in the far sanctuary wall, from which a scrawny, skeletal hand suddenly shot out.

'It's the anchorite,' Ranulf whispered. 'There is an anchorage over there.' Again the wailing screech, followed by a deep sepulchral voice.

'And the Lord sent out the Angel of Death over the Egyptians and he struck them. The Angel of Death, my Lords, is here, in this church! God's anger! Murder, I tell you!' The prophetic doom-laden voice silenced the hubbub of the sanctuary for a few seconds, then the hand disappeared. The king gestured to Bassett, the young household knight.

'Sir Fulk,' the king whispered quietly, 'clear the sanctuary and the church. Get rid of the populace here!'

The sanctuary was now being invaded by people, *domicellae*, maids of the court, knights, pages, even men-at-arms. Behind these were others: a young gallant with a hawk upon his wrist; merchants; girls with wanton looks from the streets and taverns beyond the cathedral walls. Women chattered, men talked loudly, girls whispered and laughed at the confusion which surrounded the great ones of the land.

'I will not be gaped at!' the king muttered. Across the sanctuary lay-brothers and servants of the cathedral were lifting de Montfort's body onto leather sheeting to take it out into the nearby sacristy. The king rose, turned and snapped his fingers at Corbett.

'Follow me.' He turned. 'My Lord Surrey.'

John de Warrene, Earl of Surrey, the most competent and loyal of Edward's barons, sighed and got up. The king walked across the sanctuary and past the altar, knocking aside the staring servants, priests and others still stunned by the tragedy. The king pushed under the carved-oak rood-screen, pulling aside the heavy blue velvet arras, and entered the chapel beyond, Corbett and Surrey following. The latter, white-haired and red-faced, was stroking his goatee beard. He looked as anxious and frightened as Corbett and the clerk could understand why. They had both heard the king's short but violent exchange with the archbishop and knew de Montfort's death would not help the king's cause in raising taxes from the Church. Edward walked across the empty chapel and leaned against the tomb of some long-buried bishop. Corbett, attempting to calm his mind, tried to think of the name, Erconwald, that was it! Some Saxon priest. The king, resting against the white stone sarcophagus, took deep breaths, his massive chest heaving with the strain. He glared across at his chief clerk, one of the few men he really trusted.

'I hate this church,' he rasped, looking up at the soaring roof. Corbett stared above the king at the great rose window now suffused with every colour of the rainbow as a weak sun struggled through the snow clouds.

'I hate this church,' the king whispered again. 'Here the Londoners met when they pledged their support to Simon de Montfort. Do the ghosts of Evesham dwell here?'

Corbett sensed the king's anger, taking it out on the building rather than the people it represented. Edward did have a special hatred for St Paul's, not only because of de Montfort but because it represented the lawlessness in the capital. The great bell of St Paul's would always boom out to rouse the citizens to arms, or to bring them into the great square around St Paul's Cross to hear some preacher or some rabble-rousing politician speak against the court or the king's taxes. It also had the right of sanctuary; outlaws from both sides of the river fled here from the sheriffs and other officials of the king. Edward had done his best to stop such abuses, building a huge sanctuary wall around the cathedral; but still it was more a market-place than a house of prayer. Here lawyers met their clients; servants came to be hired; merchants to arrange deals. You could buy virtually anything in this house of God.

Surrey, still stroking his beard, decided he had had enough of the king's temper.

'Are we here, Your Grace, to discuss the faults and failings of this Cathedral or,' gesturing with his head behind him to the noises behind the altar screen, 'are we here to discuss what will happen because of de Montfort's death?'

The king glared at Surrey, about to give some biting reply when he sensed he had made enough enemies, so he turned to Corbett.

'Hugh, go and see if de Montfort is truly dead. Bassett!' As Hugh turned he saw the young knight guarding the rood-screen door. Ranulf was skulking behind him, watching round-eyed at the king's anger and wondering if this would affect his fortunes and those of his master. Ranulf had been with Corbett too many times to be totally overawed by royal majesty but he sensed Edward's fickle temper and knew that if Corbett fell from favour Ranulf would also go back to the gutter from which he came. Consequently he looked after his master's happiness with an almost religious fervour. Ranulf did not want anyone to upset Corbett; he viewed that as his own prerogative.

'Basset,' the king repeated, 'go with Corbett. And Hugh,' – the king nodded to where Ranulf still skulked, 'take your watchdog with you. He should not be here.'

Corbett and Bassett bowed, pulled back the arras and went back into the hubbub in the sanctuary. Royal men-at-arms were now imposing some form of order. They had sealed the sanctuary off with a ring of steel while royal marshals and trumpeters had gone down into the nave to instruct the people to leave. Even under the noise and clamour Corbett felt the menace and threats. The people, by right, regarded the nave of the church as theirs and they resented being told to leave and so prevented from watching such an interesting spectacle. Worse, news of de Montfort's collapse and the prophetic cries of the anchorite had spread, God knows how, and the people were already muttering that de Montfort's death was a judgement against the king.

3

Corbett, followed by Bassett and Ranulf, walked across the now quietening sanctuary and entered the sacristy, a large oak-panelled room with an enormous table down the centre and aumbries in the walls. Someone had lit cresset torches and wheeled in charcoal braziers to ward off the oppressive cold. The main celebrants of the mass and the servers were still there.

Corbett gazed round the crowded sacristy. There were soldiers, guests from the service and other canons of the cathedral moving around, though they kept away from the great table now cleared except for the leather sheeting holding de Montfort's corpse. A young priest, a stole around his neck, was busy anointing the eyes, mouth and hands of the dead man. Corbett again looked round for someone in authority and finally saw a promising candidate. A youngish man of small stature, plump, with thick matted red hair, he still wore the gold and red chasuble, and Corbett recognized him as one of the main celebrants. The clerk went over to introduce himself and, when the man turned, Corbett was immediately struck by his comely and saintly face. There were some men who looked like priests, some who did not. This cleric looked every inch a man of God. His face was round and plump with deep-set blue eyes and a smooth olive skin. He smiled at Corbett.

'So, His Grace the king has sent you,' he said.

'Yes,' Corbett replied. 'I have to find out about Master

de Montfort.'

The priest turned and nodded towards where the corpse lay. 'De Montfort has gone to a different court, Master Corbett.'

'What is that priest doing?' Corbett asked.

'Anointing him.'

'I thought that only happened when a man was dying, not when he was dead.'

The priest shrugged his shoulders.

'You have read your theology, Master Clerk? Aquinas and Bonaventure say the soul may not leave the body till hours after the heart has stopped beating. For de Montfort's sake let us hope that this is so and his soul has been cleansed of sin.'

Corbett was about to go towards the table but the priest put his hand gently on the clerk's arm.

'Let the priest finish, Master Clerk,' he said. 'Then you can look.'

'And who are you?'

'I am Sir Philip Plumpton, canon of St Paul's,' the fellow replied.

Corbett nodded.

The young priest, who must also have been a celebrant at the fateful mass, had finished the anointing and now began the Psalm for the Dead: '*De Profundis Clamavi ad Le*'. Once that was ended, the young priest, head bowed so that his complete tonsure was showing, began the final invocation, telling the dead man's soul to go out, invoking the Archangels Michael and Gabriel to meet him with the heavenly host, praying the dead man's soul would not fall into the hands of the Evil One, the Son of Perdition.

Corbett shivered. Here in the house of God, surrounded by priests, he felt a malevolence, a deep-seated malice. He already half suspected that de Montfort's death was no accident and, strangely, remembered stories he had heard about St Paul's: how it was often a den of iniquity, many of the canons not following the rules of their order or the vows they made at ordination. Some people claimed it was because the cathedral had been built over an ancient temple once used by the Romans in their sacrifices to Diana, goddess of the hunt. Corbett shivered again. With evil came chaos and chaos cried out for order to be imposed. If de Montfort's death was no accident, then the king would certainly assign him to find out why.

Corbett did not relish the commission. He had already seen the king's anger and believed a great deal of it was pretence. Did Edward have a hand in de Montfort's death? The clerk had no illusions about his royal master. King Edward was a pragmatist, the means always justifying the end. In the universities of Europe there were political theorists who claimed a king was above the law; indeed, even what he wished became law. Was the corpse lying on the table proof of this? A man who came from a family hated by the king, who was preparing a speech denouncing the king's taxation. Did Edward have a hand in his death? Is that why the king himself had not come into the sacristy? Did Edward believe that the body of a murdered man always bled in the presence of his assassin?

Corbett gently removed Plumpton's hand from his wrist and walked over to the table as the young priest, his face white and lined with fear, rose and walked quietly away. The corpse, still dressed in priestly garb, had a gauze veil over its face. Corbett, now aware of the growing silence around him as people watched what he would do, removed the gauze. De Montfort's face, never handsome in life, looked tragic, almost grotesque, in death. The muscles in the face were still rigid, the eyes half open, and Corbett saw two pennies lying on either side of the head, proof that the officiating priest had attempted to lay two coins there to keep the eyes closed. Instead, they seemed to glare malevolently at Corbett: the nostrils were dilated, the lips drawn back in the awful rictus of death. Corbett, who knew a little of medicine, bent down and sniffed at the man's mouth. He detected garlic, wine and something else, a bitter-sweet smell. Steeling himself, he forced two fingers into the man's mouth and, despite the low moans of protest from the people surrounding him, gently forced the jaws open and stared in. As he suspected, the man's mouth had failed to close because the tongue had swollen and the gums round the rotting teeth were black. Corbett at once knew the truth. De Montfort had not collapsed or died; there had been no failure of the heart or sudden rush of blood to the head. De Montfort had been poisoned.

Corbett replaced the gauze veil, bowed to Plumpton and walked out of the sacristy. Bassett and Ranulf were waiting outside for him.

'What is it?' Bassett asked.

Corbett just glanced at him and walked back across the sanctuary.

Ranulf, wiping his nose noisily on the sleeve of his jerkin, relished the future; mischief was afoot and soon he and his master would be involved. They would be summoned by that high and mighty king and told to go about their secret task. If that was the case, and so far his master had never failed the king, it would mean more money, wealth and status and Ranulf would share in the reflected glory. Ranulf basked in a glow of smug self-satisfaction; the rest of London had been cleared from the nave but he, Ranulf-atte-Newgate, a former felon, a man who had been condemned to swing by the neck at the Elms, could stay. Corbett had once secured a pardon for him and, due to his master's secretive ways and sharp, clever brain, Ranulf had grown wealthy. His master, though taciturn and quiet, was always generous and Ranulf had begun to salt away a sizeable amount of gold with a goldsmith just off the Poultry. Not that Ranulf really cared for the future. He took each day as it came, his two aims being to look after Corbett and to enjoy himself as much as possible.

Ranulf's relationship with the clerk was not an easy one:

he often found his master morose and withdrawn. Sometimes Corbett would sit for hours in the corner of a tavern, sipping a cup of wine or flagon of beer, lost in his own thoughts and, if Ranulf tried to draw him, all he received were black looks. The only time Corbett seemed to come to life was in the record room amongst the piles of vellum, parchment, sealing wax, inkhorns and quills. He seemed to take as much enjoyment out of that as Ranulf did pursuing the wives and daughters of various London merchants. Of course, there was always music. In their lodgings in Bread Street, Corbett would often sit in the evening playing his flute quietly to himself, devising new tunes. There was one other reason for the clerk's quiet moods. The Welsh woman, Maeve, Corbett's betrothed, a sweet wench Ranulf thought, though he was frightened of her sharp ways and clear blue eyes. In fact, she was the only woman ever to frighten Ranulf and he half suspected Corbett himself was afeared of her. She had declared her love for his master but, so far, had refused to give a wedding date, saying affairs in Wales were still not settled following the collapse of the revolt in which her fat, wicked uncle had been deeply involved. Yes, the Welsh woman was making life arduous. Ranulf glared at his master's retreating back and, as loudly as possible, blew his nose once again on the sleeve of his jerkin. Bassett grinned, Corbett stopped mid-stride, turned and glared at his servant.

'This time,' he snapped, 'stay outside!' Ranulf smiled and nodded whilst his master, followed by Bassett, pulled back the arras of the altar-screen and rejoined the king. Edward now sat slumped in a rather unregal fashion at the foot of St Erconwald's tomb. Surrey, leaning against the wall, was busy picking his teeth, staring up at the light pouring through the rose window as if seeing it for the first time. Corbett knew his royal master was in the middle of a deep sulk. The king's long, lined face was morose, his eyes half closed as if pondering some private matter. He glanced up as Corbett entered.

'Well, clerk?'

Corbett spread his hands and shrugged. 'It is as I feared, Your Grace. Murder.'

'How do you know that?' Surrey suddenly straightened up. 'Are you a doctor, Master Clerk?'

Corbett sighed. He always feared the enmity of the great lords, men born into greatness who deeply resented anyone on whom greatness was thrust. Corbett was the king's loyal servant; he had studied hard in the colleges of Oxford, worked long hours in cold, cramped scriptoria and libraries; but his elevation had been solely due to royal favour and this was always resented by nobles like Surrey. Corbett had never yet met one nobleman who accepted him for what he was, a clever clerk, a trusted servant of the king.

Nevertheless, Corbett knew how to survive in bitter court politics.

He bowed towards Surrey. 'My Lord is correct,' he smiled ingratiatingly, although he hated himself for doing so. 'I am not a physician but I have some knowledge of poisons.'

'Then you are a rare man,' Surrey interrupted.

Corbett felt the flash of anger seep through him and he bit his lip. Was Surrey insinuating he had something to do with the priest's death? He glanced sideways at the king, who had now risen and was dusting down his robes.

'My Lord,' Corbett began again slowly, 'because of various circumstances, I know certain matters of physic, yet it is common knowledge that a man whose face is still rigid in death, with a swollen tongue and mouth as black as the hole of hell, must have been poisoned. What we must find out,' he turned and looked directly at the king, 'is who poisoned him, where and how.'

Corbett gazed into the king's eyes though he would have cheerfully loved to have turned and stared at Bassett for, when he had announced the priest had been poisoned, he had heard the knight banneret's sharp intake of breath and a muttered curse. Corbett wondered why Bassett should be so concerned. What had it to do with him? But that matter would have to wait. Corbett knew what would happen. The king would tell him to find out the reasons for de Montfort's death, and not to rest until he either found the truth or produced enough information to make it look as if the truth was known.

'Your Grace,' Corbett insisted, 'this matter must be resolved. De Montfort came from a family which everyone knows you hated. He was also a clergyman, close to his Lordship, the Archbishop of Canterbury. He intended to give a speech after this mass denouncing your intention to tax the Church.' Corbett stopped and licked his lips, but the king seemed composed, somehow drawing himself back from the black pit of anger. 'People will say,' Corbett continued, 'that de Montfort was killed by you.'

The king turned his back to Corbett, hands outstretched resting on the tomb, head bowed beneath the great rose window as if lost in some private prayer. When he turned he looked weary.

'It is true what you say, Clerk,' he said softly. 'They will place de Montfort's death, like others of his accursed family, at my door. How can I ever ask the clergy for taxes when as a body they will rise and demand justice for de Montfort's murder?' He squinted at Corbett in the poor light. 'But how?'

'Two ways,' Corbett replied suddenly, almost without thinking. 'Either he was poisoned before mass began or –'

'Or what?' the king snapped.

'Or,' Corbett said quietly, 'the chalice was poisoned.'

Corbett saw even the king's face go pale at the blasphemy he had uttered.

'You mean,' Surrey interjected, 'that the wine, the consecrated wine, Christ's blood, was poisoned by somebody? Then it must have been someone who celebrated mass.'

The earl came across the room and stared into Corbett's eyes.

'You realize what you are saying, Clerk? That a priest or canons of this church, in the middle of mass, the most sacred of ceremonies, poisoned the consecrated chalice and gave it to de Montfort to drink?'

'I do,' Corbett replied, gazing back steadily. He turned towards where the king stood. 'I urge Your Grace to order a guard placed round the high altar and that none of the chalices or patens or anything else be removed until we have examined them.'

The king nodded and muttered a quiet command to Bassett, who bustled from the room.

'This is clever,' the king said slowly. 'Whatever happens, we must be careful. Do we accept de Montfort's death and protest our innocence, for we *are* innocent, or investigate it? If the latter, each of those canons must be interrogated, which might cause a public scandal – and still we could find nothing. Indeed, we could be accused of trying to put the blame on innocent people.' The king chewed his lower lip and ran a beringed hand through his steel-grey hair. He took off his chaplet of silver and laid it unceremoniously on top of the tomb. 'What do you advise, Surrey?'

'Let sleeping dogs lie!' the earl answered quickly. 'Leave it alone, Your Grace!'

'Corbett?'

'I would agree with my Lord of Surrey,' Corbett replied. 'But there is one thing we have forgotten.'

'What is that?'

'The chalice,' Corbett replied. 'Do you remember, my Lord? You were to receive communion under both kinds. We must ask ourselves, was the chalice poisoned for de Montfort to drink? Or, Your Grace, was it poisoned for you?'

The king rubbed his face in his hands and looked up at the gargoyles above the stone dog's-tooth tracery. Corbett followed his gaze. There, angels jutted out of the walls, their cheeks puffed to blow the last trumpet; beside them, the faces of demons, eyes protuberant, tongues lashing out perpetually in stone. Beneath these gargoyles, in a glorious array of purples, golds, reds and blues, was a painting of heaven: a golden paradise where souls of the blessed in white robes armed with golden harps sang to a Christ eternally in judgement, while beneath their feet, in a hellish haze of red and brown, scaled demons with the heads of monsters and the bodies of lions put the souls of the damned through unspeakable tortures. Corbett watched the king take all this in. Surrey, bored by what was going on, leaned against a wall and stared down at the ground as if he had nothing to add to Corbett's conclusions. The king walked over to the clerk, so close Hugh could smell the mixture of perfume and sweat from the heavy, gold-encrusted robes.

'In this church, Hugh,' the king said softly, ignoring Surrey's presence as of no consequence, 'lies the body of another English king, Ethelred the Unready. The sword was never far from his house and all the heavens seemed to rage against him. Is that to be my fate?'

Corbett could have felt some sympathy but as he watched the light blue eyes of the king, he wondered again whether Edward, the most consummate of actors, was simply allaying his own fears.

'This murder must be resolved,' the king continued. 'Not because of de Montfort's death,' – he almost snapped the words out, 'I wish him good riddance and others of his ilk. But if someone intended to kill me, Corbett, I want him found.'

'If that is so, Your Grace,' Corbett replied quickly, eager to escape this baleful royal presence, 'it is best if I examine the altar and the chalice. You agree?'

The king nodded. 'Go. We shall wait for you here.'

4

Corbett re-entered the sanctuary. The candles had been extinguished and the church cleared. In the far corner, Winchelsea and his host, the Bishop of London, stood in close conversation with Bohun and Bigod. Other nobles and ecclesiastical dignitaries stood round, their faces full of false concern, as if they had taken the events of that morning as a personal shock. A few canons stood gaping at the high altar now ringed by royal men-at-arms, who would allow no one through. Most of the people had left, though the drama of the morning's events the singing, the chants and the dreadful death hung as heavy in the air as the fragrant clouds of incense.

Corbett stopped, noticing a figure at the foot of the sanctuary steps. It was a woman dressed in a kirtle of white and gold damask and a mantle of the same material, trimmed with ermine and fastened around her shoulders by great lace bows of gold and silk, each with its rich knob of gold tassel. Her fair hair hung down her back, held in place by a thin, silken net studded with gems. Her face was long and smooth, almost regal if it hadn't been for the bold eyes and the sly twist of her mouth. Corbett had never seen her before. At first he thought she may have been a lady of the court but he looked closer at the painted lips and nails and dismissed her as a high-class courtesan, maybe a mistress of one of the great ones still standing in the sanctuary, or even that of a canon of the church. Corbett wryly remembered the old proverb: the cowl doesn't make the monk; many priests were as ardent for the ways of flesh as they were when they preached publicly against the same sins in their pulpits. Corbett was about to turn away when the woman suddenly called out in a rather harsh voice.

'Is de Montfort dead?'

Corbett turned and, before he could think, replied,

'Yes, the fellow is dead.' By the time he had regained his composure, the woman had spun on her heel and walked boldly down the nave of the church, her broad rich hips swaying suggestively under the silken gown. Corbett would have liked to go after her and ask why she was so interested, but the king was waiting, so he turned and walked up the line of men-at-arms. As he approached, one of them put out a hand to stop him, but Bassett, hurrying behind, had a whispered conversation with the Captain of the Guard and Corbett was allowed through.

He strode up the main steps and stood at the altar. It was long, broader than Corbett had thought, and made of marble. Its frontal was covered with intricate carvings of angels and shepherds, a scene treated with almost childish gaiety; the shepherd was blowing so loud a blast upon his bagpipe he could not hear the heavenly song. Corbett looked at the carving, touching its smoothness, forgetting for the moment the task in hand as he admired its intricate, carefully carved tracery. He crouched down and looked at the faint wine stain and noticed that similar red blotches stained the carpet. Had wine been spilt? It seemed a little had. He shrugged and rose to scrutinize the altar itself, placing his hands on it, feeling beneath the linen, now covered in pools of pure wax, the precious cloths which, he suspected, were sendal, samite, sarcanet, damask silk and velvet. The top cloth itself pure white with embroidery around the edges in tawny brown, gold, green and deep blue. In the centre of the linen cloth was a red cross which marked the relic stone every altar bore but because this was the cathedral of St Paul's, it covered some of the rarest relics: a splinter of the true cross, grains from a stone on which Christ had stood before he ascended into heaven, a piece of the Virgin's veil and relics from St Paul's tomb in Rome.

On the altar stood beautiful jewel-work: huge candlesticks, a mass of writhing, intertwining, silver foliage, adorned with tiny gold figures of men and demons; small shallow cruets with stems of coloured crystal engraved with scenes from the Passion of Christ. There was a many-rayed monstrance, patens of pale, beautiful silver gilt, some still holding consecrated hosts. A gold-encrusted thurible had also been left there in the confusion and beside it a jewel-covered, boat-shaped incense-carrier. Corbett scrutinized all of these carefully. Many priests would consider him guilty of blasphemy, for the sacred bread and wine were still on the altar, but Corbett believed he knew enough of theology to realize blasphemy is what one intends, not what one does. He murmured a short prayer, struck his breast again, muttering '*Peccavi*,' believing God would see into his heart and realize he meant no disrespect but was pursuing the truth; for surely, here, a terrible crime had been committed? But how?

Corbett went through the rite of the mass. After the *Agnus Dei*, all the celebrants would take a host from the silver patens on the altar: Then the chalice would be taken up, each celebrant taking a sip before passing it on to his fellow. Is this how de Montfort had been poisoned? Corbett walked towards the thurible and picked up the gold cap; inside the small charcoal pieces were now cold. Corbett sniffed but smelt nothing except burnt incense. The wild fantasy occurred to him that perhaps de Montfort had been killed by breathing some deadly fume, but he dismissed it. If de Montfort had smelt it, so had others in the church; yet they were hale and hearty while de Montfort lay dead in the sacristy, his body going rigid in death. Had the host been poisoned? Corbett rejected the idea. After all, no priest would know which host would be given to him and that did not fit into his suspicion of the king being the intended victim rather than de Montfort. It must have been the wine.

Corbett walked over to the solitary chalice, still half full with wine. He picked it up and smelt it, but could only detect the fragrant tang of grape. He put a finger in and was about to taste when a voice suddenly shouted out, 'That is blasphemy!'

He turned to find that Winchelsea, his face pale with fury, had come to the bottom of the altar steps and was glaring through the ranks of soldiers at Corbett.

'What are you doing, man?'

'My Lord Bishop,' Corbett replied, 'I do nothing except on the king's orders. De Montfort was poisoned at this altar. I mean no blasphemy but somewhere here lies the venom which killed him. If we can find that then we can expose the poisoner.' Corbett looked at the archbishop glaring at him.

'You have no right. You are a layperson,' the Archbishop snapped. 'You should have my permission or at least that of his Lordship, the Bishop of London, before you even approach the altar.'

'My Lord Bishop,' Corbett said, tired of the farce of speaking over the shoulders of the men-at-arms, some of whom were grinning broadly at the altercation. 'My Lord Bishop, if you object to what I am doing, then see the king. Or, if you wish, excommunicate me. Yet I mean no disrespect. On this altar lies the source of de Montfort's death and I intend to find it.'

'The clerk is right,' another voice broke in and Corbett turned to see Plumpton at the far corner of the altar gazing up at him. 'My Lord Bishop,' Plumpton continued smoothly, 'the clerk means no disrespect. He is here on the king's orders. There is enough tension in this church. Now, perhaps if I assisted him?'

The archbishop nodded and Plumpton waddled up the

steps past the soldiers and joined Corbett in the centre of the altar.

'Have you found the poison, Master Clerk?'

'I have found nothing,' Corbett said, turning his back on the still fuming prelate. 'This is the principal chalice?' He picked up the beautifully engraved cup.

'That is the only chalice,' Plumpton replied. 'It belonged to de Montfort. He was very proud of it. After all, it was given to him by the great Earl Simon himself.'

'And he drank from this?'

Plumpton nodded.

'Then this was the source of his death.'

Plumpton took the brimming cup and drained it before placing it back on the altar. 'I do not think so,' he said. 'I have drunk the consecrated wine because someone had to and, in a few minutes, you will find out if it was poisoned. I think, Master Clerk,' he smiled at Corbett, 'you already know that. The chalice is not poisoned. Remember we all drank from it at mass.'

Corbett chewed his lower lip and nodded. He could find nothing here. 'Sir priest,' he said, 'thank you for your help. I meant no disrespect.' Corbett gestured with his hand. 'I realize the priests here must clean and tidy the altar but I order you now, and this is from the king himself, none of this must be removed from the church until it has been examined again.'

Plumpton shrugged his shoulders. 'Of course. But,' he said, 'I understand the king waits for you now. My Lord Bishop of London has prepared a banquet for us to celebrate the king's discomfiture but the cooks are ready and de Montfort's death has surely not spoilt our appetite.'

Corbett grinned, passed through the ranks of soldiers down the altar steps, gazed coolly at the still glowering archbishop and walked back behind the rood-screen to join the king. He found Edward had regained his composure and allowed in others of the royal household: marshals, stewards, courtiers, all bustling around, attempting to impose some order on the chaos which had broken out. The king had a silver ewer of water and napkins brought to him. He washed his hands with fragrant soap and allowed the royal barber to comb his beard and hair and replace the silver chaplet. Once that was done, Edward announced that His Grace the Bishop of London awaited them in the chapter-house and, followed by a trail of retainers, Corbett and Surrey included, the king strode back into the sanctuary. He ignored the others standing there and, walking out of the east door, went through the windswept snow-covered cloisters and into the chapter-house of the cathedral.

The white plaster walls of the great chapter-house were covered in costly Flemish tapestries and thick Persian carpets had been laid on the polished oaken floor. Candelabra of thick silver, each with a pure wax candle, kept away the darkness. There were braziers full of charcoal on small wheels; fresh herbs had been placed on them before their steel caps were fixed and they were wheeled into the room.

In the far wall a huge fire roared, fed with sea coal and fresh pine logs and at the end of the hall, on a dais under a heavy rafter beam draped with red, white and gold hangings, stood the great table; behind it, carved oaken chairs. The table itself was covered by a white cloth and bedecked with silver and gold ornaments. The canons had evidently raided their treasury, removing all the precious ornaments to grace the hall and so awe the king. Corbett wondered if it was meant as a quiet jest at Edward's expense. He would have heard de Montfort's tirade against royal taxation and then been brought here and feasted at the church's expense, the bishops and canons taunting him with the treasures they so avidly denied him. The king, as if realizing the joke intended for him, did not wait for others to join him from the cathedral, but strode to the head of the hall and took the main seat on the dais. After that it was a frenetic scramble for places, people jostling to be as close as possible to the royal table on the dais. Corbett did not mind. The king had asked him to stay but Corbett whispered it would be better if he dined in the body of the hall and listened to any rumours or whispers which were circulating. The king had nodded. Corbett however realized that Edward, if he was the object of someone's malice, was as vulnerable here as he was in church.

'Your Grace,' he murmured, 'had best be careful what he eats or drinks.'

Surrey, who had placed himself at the king's left hand, turned angrily to Corbett. 'You need not worry, clerk,' he snapped. 'The king will not eat or drink what I have not eaten or drunk first.'

'Then my Lord,' Corbett replied coolly, 'knowing His Grace's life is in your hands and I have your word for it, I feel safe.' He bowed towards the king and withdrew, leaving Surrey, not the most nimble-witted of Edward's courtiers, to wonder if an insult had been given or not.

Corbett chose his place carefully. Already he had suspicions about Plumpton – far too gracious, far too pleasant, almost happy and relieved to see de Montfort dead. A man, Corbett considered, who needed questioning. So when people took their places, he slipped quietly onto the bench beside Plumpton. The canon, apparently pleased by his company, soon engaged him in a detailed conversation about the history of the cathedral whilst carefully avoiding any reference to de Montfort's death. Corbett listened carefully, though wondering where Bassett and Ranulf were. Ranulf, unable to find a seat in the hall, was quick-witted enough to know he would be served better and faster if he went into the kitchens, claiming to be a royal retainer; while Bassett would undoubtedly be carrying out some secret errand of the king. As Plumpton talked, Corbett thought of Bassett, a young man, a knight banneret probably from a landed family. Corbett had met such young men before: they were becoming ever more popular at the court, were totally devoted to the king and seemed to embody that dreadful legal maxim, 'The will of the Prince is force of law.' Bassett was one of these. A ruthlessly ambitious young man for whom there was no morality, no right or wrong, no heaven or hell, no grace no sin, no good no evil, nothing but the will of the prince.

As the king grew older he seemed to surround himself with such men, for Edward could never brook opposition even as a young man, and in his old age found it, however slight, totally intolerable. Corbett had seen Edward fight in Wales. There the king had shown magnanimity to defeated rebels, but now? Corbett looked up the long hall to where the king sat in regal splendour at the high table. Now it was different. Corbett had heard about the expedition to Scotland, the sheer butchery, the king's murderous intent. Men like Surrey who sat beside the king were simply an extension of this royal fury. Surrey was an able soldier, a veteran warrior. He would put a town to the torch as easily as he would cross a street or mount a horse. Sometimes Corbett wondered whether he should serve the king; he had done well with estates in Sussex and was the proud owner of tenements in Suffolk, Shotters Brook, Clerkenwell and Bread Street. He thought of a phrase in the gospel, 'What does it profit a man if he gain the whole world but lose his own soul?' Corbett had to walk gingerly in the intricate politics of the English court, where it would be so easy for a man to lose his way and, eventually, his soul.

The present case was no different. Corbett believed the chalice may have been meant for de Montfort but he had remembered the conversation before mass when Bassett had reminded the king (Corbett had been seated behind him) how, after the priest had taken the chalice as a gesture of friendship, the same cup would be brought for the king to drink. But who would want to kill Edward? Corbett sighed. There must be hundreds. Philip of France,

Edward's sworn enemy, would be only too pleased to see the king die in his cups, or collapse before the high altar in his principal cathedral. Philip would then announce to Christendom how it was God's judgement on a perfidious English king. There were the Welsh chieftains, rebellious and seething with treachery. Corbett had dealt with such; that was how he had met Maeve ... her sweet diamond-shaped face framed by long silver-blonde hair flickered into his mind. Corbett closed his eyes and removed the vision. If he started thinking about Maeve nothing would be done. Finally, of course, there were the Scots. Corbett had met their chieftains, Bruce and others, ruthless men totally determined not to give one inch of Scottish soil to England.

Maeve's smiling face returned, so Corbett asserted himself by gazing round the hall. The meal was being served; the Bishop of London's cooks, despite the season, had done their best to provide a banquet. Baked mallard, teal, small birds served in almond milk, capon roasted in syrup, roasted veal, roasted pig, herons, tartar flesh, jellies, broiled rabbit, pheasant, venison, even hedgehogs skinned and baked in a rich sauce, cranes, partridges, custards, oranges, sweet *doucettes* all served up by a myriad of retainers. They were equally generous in filling the pewter cups from flagons of rich red wine. Corbett, despite his long fast, did not feel hungry. He still remembered de Montfort's face, the blackened mouth and swollen tongue. Moreover, in the far corner of the hall he had just seen a cat carrying the half-gnawed body of a rat and this, together with some of the gaping ulcers on the arms and hands of several of the serving boys, had decidedly put him off his meal. So he sipped quietly at the wine, vowing that as soon as the banquet was over, he would make his way into the city to justify his own hunger.

Plumpton was still talking and Corbett let him babble on as he carefully examined his wooden platter or roundel, tracing with his finger certain verses of the Bible inscribed on it in gilt lettering. This was indeed wealth. The canons of St Paul's may not have known much of poverty but they certainly did about wealth. Even in a nobleman's house the roundel or trancher would have held stale bread, but here it was different. Even the cups given to them were of pewter. Their meals had been served on silver and gold dishes; the candles on the table were pure wax; the drapes on the wall were thick and heavily encrusted with gold. No stone floor, but polished wood covered with carpets. Charcoal braziers, the black metal polished clean, glowed red, giving off not only heat but a sweet fragrance. Plumpton, beside him, sat dressed in a thick robe and cowl lined with white ermine, his fleshy hands covered in rings. Corbett almost recoiled at the womanish perfume the man emanated. The priest seemed oblivious to this as he described the workings of the cathedral until Corbett, tired, decided to interrupt.

'Sir Philip,' he said softly, 'who would want de Montfort dead?'

Plumpton turned, his face beaming with pleasure. 'I for one.'

'You did not like the dean?'

'No,' he said, 'I did not like the dean, a mysterious, strange man. I would have liked his post, the office of dean. It should have been mine anyway.'

Corbett was slightly taken aback at such a disclosure.

'And how many more disliked him?'

Plumpton spread his hands and gazed around. 'The cathedral is a small city in itself. There is the bishop, the dean, the treasurer, the sacrist, the almoner, the librarian. We have our servants, those who clean the church, those who serve us here. Our huntsmen, our washerwomen, our messengers, our tailors. I don't think you'd find one who liked Master de Montfort or who is going to weep copious tears because he is dead.'

Plumpton sipped from his cup and peered closely at Corbett. 'And you, Master Clerk, do you think it was an accident? I have heard say you announced it as murder. It is murder, is it not.'

'What do you think?' Corbett asked. 'Who would murder the Dean of St Paul's?'

Plumpton grinned again.

'Why not ask your master, the king,' he said.

Corbett placed his hand firmly on Plumpton's arm. 'Sir priest,' he said, 'some men would say that was treason.'

Plumpton slowly removed Corbett's hand. 'Some men, Master Clerk, say it is the truth.' He gazed steadily at Corbett. 'Why not ask your king? After all, was it not Bassett who brought a flagon of wine, the best Bordeaux, as a gift from your royal master, just before mass began?'

Corbett stared back. 'I did not know that.'

'There are many things that you did not know,' the priest replied peevishly. He suddenly raised a beringed hand and snapped his fingers. A servant, one eye covered by a black patch, shuffled forward. Corbett looked at him, the emaciated face, the long lank hair, the greasy leather jerkin and canvas apron tied around his waist.

'Simon,' the priest said softly, 'is my servant. Simon has something to show you.' He whispered into the servant's ear, the man nodded and shuffled away.

Corbett turned back to the table where around him the general hum of conversation was unbroken; people ignored him, intent on filling their own bellies and acquiring some warmth against the savage cold outside. The wine was now circulating freely and already some of the canons looked the worse for wear, bleary-eyed and droop-mouthed. Corbett knew the king would stay here most of the day, intent on showing he had nothing to hide or fear, and would be only too willing to relax and feast himself on the riches of the Church. Corbett would have liked to go but waited until the servant reappeared. In one hand he carried a cup, in the other a leather pannikin of wine. Corbett looked at the cup, which was empty: a simple design, made of good-quality pewter. The pannikin was of leather lined with gilt; the stopper of hard-boiled polished leather fitted the top snugly. Corbett had seen many such used around the royal palace. He looked at the cup, sniffing at the brim and caught a faint but strange smell. He then uncorked the pannikin of wine and the bitter sweet smell almost made him choke. Plumpton watched in amusement.

'They are yours, Master Clerk. That smell, this morning in the sacristy, it is the same now. I am sure, Master Clerk,' Plumpton continued smoothly, 'that if you took a gulp of that, you would not leave this hall alive. But they are yours. I give them as a free gift, for in the wrong hands they could well be used as a weapon against the king.'

Corbett nodded. 'I will not forget,' he said. He replaced the stopper carefully, making sure it was screwed in tightly, rose and without a word to Plumpton or his shadowy servant, walked from the hall, with both cup and pannikin concealed beneath his robe.

5

Corbett walked out of the warm chapter-house and into the icy cold cloisters. It was now bitterly cold; the sun had set and a grey dusk was closing in. Flurries of snow fell, adding a fresh carpet to what had come before. An unnatural stillness hung over the cathedral grounds, as if the snow had blanketed everything under a canopy of peace; yet Corbett knew different. Only two years ago the king had ordered a high wall to be erected around the cathedral, strengthened by gates which were locked every night and opened only when the bells rang for prime. Here were men who had fled from the law, seeking sanctuary: the scum of London, broken men declared '*utlegatum*' – beyond the law. They came here untroubled by royal officers or other city officials. Through the falling flakes, across the graves and mounds now hidden by the snow, Corbett could see the great stone wall and the makeshift shelters erected against it. Men, women and children, faint figures swathed in skins and rags, like those in a nightmare, slipped silently by. He saw the dim glow of fires and heard the cry of a baby, painful against the encroaching freezing night. A hopeless scene. The grounds were taken up by the dead and used by those who lived in a sort of half-dead state.

A dreadful place, Corbett concluded, it evoked the old demons in his soul. He remembered a friend, an Arab physician whom he had once met years ago in London, talk of a sickness of the soul which excited the base humours of the body; the mind became clouded and eventually it led to suicide. Corbett thought such a nightmare always awaited him, that he would settle in some black fit of depression and, unable to continue, simply lie down and die. The graveyards and grounds of the Cathedral of St Paul's evoked these demons: here, in Christ's house, where Christ lived, his figure perpetually crucified, the priests fed like pigs, their bodies, sleek, fat, plump, clothed and warm; while the poor, like the cat he had seen earlier, squatted where they could, eating what they had scavenged.

Corbett passed a group of horses tethered together, waiting for their masters to finish their feasting, the grooms long since disappeared. Corbett rounded a corner and entered the south door of the cathedral. On either side of the gloomy entrance were small wooden iron-barred gates leading to the tower. Corbett ensured these were fastened. He didn't know why, but he simply did not want to pass a door which might be open, for he could not shake off a feeling of evil, of watchful malice. He walked up into the nave. On either side of him the transepts were shrouded in darkness, the stout rounded pillars standing like a row of silent guardians, thrusting the mass of stone, as if by magic, up into the air. The place was deserted. Usually, this market-place of London would be packed by scribes, lawyers, parchment-sellers, and servants. Here men would come to talk of lawsuits and crop prices; women had neighbourly chats even while divine service was being celebrated, sometimes only becoming quiet when the host was elevated. St Paul's was a useful meeting-place where enemies might confer on safe ground; arbitrators decide a land quarrel; a young man with marriage on his mind arrange to meet a young girl and her family.

Corbett jumped as the great bell of St Paul's began booming out, a sign that the curfew would be imposed, the gates locked and chains laid across them to deny access to any of the roaring gangs of lawless youths who terrorized the city at night. It was cold, deathly cold. Corbett walked on past the small, shadowy embrasures where the chancery priests sang masses for those who paid money to escape God's judgement for their sins on earth. He climbed the steps into the choir; on either side the wooden stalls were empty, the carved gargoyles staring in motionless terror towards him. Wall torches still spluttered faintly, throwing deep shadows and giving the patterned stone-work a life of its own. Corbett entered the silent sanctuary. Here too, torches fixed into their iron sockets in the wall provided a little light. Corbett looked up at the high altar which had been cleared. The sacred vessels were now covered with a thick, dark cloth, though the incense from the morning mass still hung in the air like souls who refused to ascend to heaven.

The high altar with its carved frontal was now shrouded in virtual darkness, except for the solitary red winking sanctuary light which shone through the gloom like a beacon in a storm. Corbett remembered the words carved on the wooden sanctuary screen he had just passed through. '*Hic locus terribilis. Dominus Dei et porta coeli*' – This is indeed a terrible place, the house of God and the gate of heaven. Corbett shivered. Perhaps it was also the gate of hell. Here Christ dwelt under the appearance of bread and wine, surrounded by a horde of adoring angels, the whole might of heaven's armies. But was that true? Corbett could hardly believe it. Did what the priest say really exist? Was it true? Were some philosophers right when they said that man lived in a world of simple appearances? Did Corbett constantly dwell in the shadows unaware of the true reality beyond it? Or, as St Augustine put it, was man a mere child playing in the rock pools of a beach ignoring the great ocean whispering beside him? Yet there was a reality here, even if it was just the reality of evil. Corbett found it difficult to believe that this cathedral, founded on the ruins of an ancient Roman temple, was really a holy place.

Here, after all, a priest had been murdered, struck down as he prepared to meet Christ himself. Was it God's dreadful judgement on that man? And what more terrible judgement would await those who had planned such a hideous crime?

Corbett jumped. He heard a sound from the far sanctuary wall; drawing his dagger from beneath his cloak he walked softly over, his heart pounding, his mouth becoming so dry that his tongue was rigid between his teeth. The scraping seemed to come out of the wall itself. Corbett, the sweat now breaking out on his body, placed his hand gingerly on the wall and began to feel down to where the sound had come from. Suddenly his shuffling fingers were caught in an icy vice-like grip. The clerk raised his other hand but his palm, wet with sweat, let the dagger slip with a clang onto the flagstone. Corbett tried to curb his rising panic. He saw a ray of light appear in the wall and moaned in terror. Had one of the stone devils, the grinning gargoyles high up the wall, unexpectedly come to life and in this evil place slithered down serpent-like to seize him? Corbett panicked and he was on the point of screaming when he heard the voice.

'Are you from God or the Devil?' it whispered through the slit of light.

'From God! From God!' Corbett shouted back, trying to compose himself. He had forgotten about the anchorite. The man must have heard him enter the sanctuary and Corbett had blundered into his trap. Was this man the murderer? he thought wildly.

'Let go of my hand!' he yelled. 'By God, if you do not let me go, I will stab you.'

'I heard your dagger fall,' the voice whispered in reply. 'But I wish you no ill. I will let your hand go.'

Corbett suddenly felt his fingers free. He jumped away from the wall, felt for his dagger and retreated slowly backwards.

'Who are you?' he asked, addressing the thin ray of light

which beamed down from behind the stonework.

'I am a man of God,' the voice replied. 'My name is Thomas. I have dwelt here, oh, ten, fifteen years. You are the clerk,' he stated.

'How do you know?'

'I saw you this morning when the priest died, scurrying backwards and forwards across the sanctuary. Oh, a man of the world, deep in its affairs. Do you know how the priest died?'

Corbett sheathed his knife and tried to control the trembling in his limbs.

'The priest was murdered. You know that.' Corbett taunted. 'Was it not you who cried out the Angel of Death was visiting this place? How did you know that?'

The ray of light seemed to fade and Corbett, squinting through the darkness, could just make out a pair of eyes smiling behind the slit in the wall.

'There was no vision,' the voice chuckled. 'If you had seen, Master Clerk, what I have seen in this place, then it was only a matter of time before God sent his angel to wreak vengeance.'

'Why?' Corbett asked.

'Why?' the voice rose. 'These canons, these priests, they gabble through the mass; the Devil must collect what they miss out from the Divine Service and put it into his bag, so that when these priests die they will spend an eternity going through the services they have missed, the prayers they have omitted, the sermons they have forgotten. God's word is hurried, hurled away like one throws rubbish into a pit. And the lives they lead! You saw the whores?'

Corbett remembered the woman he had seen at the foot of the sanctuary steps.

'Yes,' he replied. 'I saw the woman.'

'A whore,' the voice retorted. 'De Montfort's whore.'

'You mean the priest who died.'

'The priest who was murdered,' the anchorite's voice was firm. 'You know that, Master Clerk. Oh, I have heard the gossip. I may dwell here, a prisoner of stone, and I do so willingly to atone for my own sins, but I see the sins of others and de Montfort was a sinner. The woman was his whore.'

'Do you know her name?'

'Her name is Legion,' the anchorite replied, 'for she has many devils in her. Ask around. De Montfort was a wealthy, acquisitive man.'

'The king,' Corbett said, suddenly trusting the anchorite, 'has told me to investigate the reasons behind this priest's death.'

The anchorite laughed, the sound pouring out of the stonework. 'There are as many reasons for de Montfort's death as stars in the heavens. Surely he had many enemies!'

'How do you know that?'

'Where do you think, Master Clerk, men come to conspire and plot? Where safer than in the sanctuary of God's own house? De Montfort was no different. But I tell you this most solemnly, Clerk, then I will not speak again to you. De Montfort was killed by his own brethren, here, in the cathedral of St Paul's. In this stewhouse, you will find men more evil than de Montfort, priests who have sold their souls to the Devil. I wish you luck!'

Suddenly the ray of light was extinguished. Corbett realized the anchorite had blown out the candle and would speak no more to him. He heard a rattling in the wall as the anchorite placed a piece of wood or rock in the gap, sealing himself off from the world.

Corbett walked away from the anchorage, back into the centre of the sanctuary and up the broad steps to the high altar. Once again he felt the dreadful stillness return. He placed his hands on the altar, bowed to the crucifix which hung above it and stared around. He tried to picture what de Montfort must have felt. He was standing here above the sanctuary stone; on either side of him stood those concelebrating the mass. The *Agnus Dei* was over and the host elevated. Other particles of sacred bread, which each of the officiating priests ate, passed along the altar on silver patens; then the chalice was passed around. Did this hold the poison? Corbett had seen Plumpton drink it himself. There had been nothing there. Others had drunk from it as well with no ill effects. But, if there was no poison in the chalice, how did de Montfort die? Was Plumpton correct? Was he looking in the wrong place?

Corbett felt the wineskin beneath his cloak; he had fastened it to his belt where it swung lightly against his leg. Was de Montfort poisoned before the service began? Corbett bit his lip and looked down towards the sacristy door: heavy, wooden, padlocked. Behind that lay de Montfort's body, now rigid and stinking in death, soaked in the poison he had drunk. Corbett thought back. The service had ended just before midday, before the great bell of St Paul's pealed out for nones. It had begun two hours beforehand. If de Montfort had drunk the poisoned wine before mass, it would have been at what hour, nine, ten o'clock in the morning? But would it take so long?

Perhaps Surrey was right; perhaps the matter should be left alone. Was he following some will-o'-the-wisp across a treacherous marsh? But surely there was an answer. Perhaps somebody, some rival had poisoned the wine the king had sent to de Montfort to get rid of this priest, the poison not acting immediately but later during the service?

Corbett sat on the top sanctuary step and thought quickly. There were three things wrong with this. First, despite his many distractions during the service, never once had he seen de Montfort falter or stumble. Nothing strange had been noticed during the mass. Surely a man who was being slowly poisoned would complain of pains? But no such thing had happened. Secondly, if this poison was given before mass, it must have been a very slow-acting one. Yet Corbett, in all his experience, had never heard of this. Most poisons were deadly swift. As a clerk in the King's Bench, he had attended the trial of many accused of poisoning; such poisons acted within minutes. Indeed, that was how the culprit was often apprehended: he or she could never leave the place of the crime quickly enough. Thirdly, and here Corbett was glad he knew a little of Canon Law, any priest who was saying mass and receiving the sacrament, could not eat or drink after midnight. It would be ridiculous to think de Montfort had drunk the wine the evening before, the poison not acting until many hours later.

Corbett frowned in concentration, baffled at the mystery. Whoever had planned de Montfort's murder had plotted it carefully. But why here? Why, if someone wanted to kill de Montfort, do it in the open before the eyes of the king, his court, the chief officers of the crown, and most of the leading dignitaries of London? Indeed, the same mystery surrounded any would-be assassin's attempt to kill the king. Why here in St Paul's at the sacrifice of the mass? Corbett rubbed his eyes; he was exhausted, weary of this matter. He got up and walked back down the nave. He heard a sound, a faint scuffling in the transept. Corbett stopped, feeling the panic and fear return. If he went out there, anyone, virtually a whole army, could hide in the darkness. Yet if someone had wanted to kill him they could have struck when he sat in the pool of light in the sanctuary. Was it just a trick of his imagination? Corbett strode quickly on, almost shouting with relief as he opened the door and stepped into the snowy whiteness outside the cathedral.

6

The next morning Corbett was awake long before the bells of the city churches began to toll for prime. It was a grey, misty morning and more snow had fallen during the night. Corbett, who could now afford to have his windows glazed, was glad he had fitted new wooden shutters, a second barrier against the ever piercing wind. His chamber was simple, albeit spacious and the plaster walls were covered with worsted hangings of red, green and blue. A large oaken cupboard kept cups and a collection of plate. There was a table-board over a pair of trestles, a bench, a stool, a heavy carved high-backed chair with arms and scarlet cushion. Corbett had cleared the floor of rushes and straw, those harbourers of dirt and disease, and spent precious gold on a thick heavy Persian carpet, an object of envy to his few visitors. Most of the room was taken up with the broad oak-carved bed, now draped with a dark blue coverlet and surrounded by heavy serge curtains, there not only to maintain privacy but also a protection against the biting cold.

Corbett had already lit the charcoal brazier, ever anxious lest a spark escape and start a fire. He took the same care with a chafing-dish set on a table to heat the room and a silver candelabra which bore four candles, each of which now flickered, giving off some meagre warmth and light. From beneath the bed Corbett pulled an iron-studded trunk and, undoing the locks, pulled out his warmest shirts, robes, leggings and a stout pair of walking boots. He also took out a belt he had owned since the Welsh wars and, pulling out another trunk, slipped a long wicked Welsh dagger and a thin rapier into two sheaths. He crossed to the laver stand holding a basin and towels and washed his face and hands, quietly cursing the cold. Once finished, he secured the trunk, pushing it back under the bed, extinguished the fire and lights and, looking once more around his chamber, left, going up a further flight of stairs to a small room beneath the roof where Ranulf slept.

His servant's garret was totally disordered and Corbett grinned mirthlessly. He remembered the previous night, tramping round most of St Paul's looking for his servant, only to find him drunk as a stoat in one of the outer kitchens. Ranulf had gorged himself on the leavings of the feast and drunk flagon after flagon of wine, openly boasting about his own greatness and the silver he might give to a pretty kitchen maid he was inveigling into spending the night with him. Cursing and yelling he had been dragged by Corbett out into the cold, along the dark narrow alleyways back to Bread Street. Ranulf had threatened his master, accusing him of being a summoner and refusing him any pleasures. Corbett had dragged him along, brutally ignoring his protestations. Only twice did he stop: once to allow Ranulf to be sick; the other to douse him in a horse trough. The icy-cold water had helped to bring Ranulf to his senses, though by the time they had reached Bread Street, Ranulf had fallen into a stupor and his master had to drag him up the stairs and toss him onto his trestle bed.

Corbett had warned him time and again not to drink to excess and to watch his tongue. Now he would emphasize the lesson. He picked up an ewer of ice-cold water and poured it slowly over Ranulf's tousled head. The servant woke gasping, spluttering, cursing and, if it had not been for the look in Corbett's eyes, Ranulf would certainly have struck the clerk full in the face.

'You are, Master Clerk,' he rasped through clenched teeth, 'a most cruel man.'

'And you Master Ranulf,' Corbett jibed in reply, 'are a most stupid man. I have ordered you on a number of occasions, whenever we are on the king's business to watch what you drink, because if your tongue wags when it shouldn't, it may well cost us our lives, not to mention being arrested by serjeants of the king's court on some charge of treason!'

Corbett jerked Ranulf roughly out of bed. The fellow was still fully dressed except for his boots, and Corbett made his servant sit on the edge of the bed and threw them at him.

'Put them on!' he ordered. 'Go downstairs. Relieve yourself in the street. Your stomach must be a cesspit now. I will not have you stinking the house out with your stale humours.'

Ranulf pulled on his boots, glared at the dark, tense face of his master and the narrow green cat-like eyes, and decided that revenge could wait. He would bide his time and wait for his ever-sombre master to become maudlin-drunk in some tavern and serve back the same medicine. Ranulf clattered downstairs.

A little later, rather pleased he had followed Corbett's advice, Ranulf returned; but his master had not yet finished. He ordered Ranulf back up to his room to strip and wash and put on a fresh change of clothing. Only then, when both of them were dressed in woollen hose, long high boots, surcoat and hood, did they venture downstairs into the street.

Corbett had decided not to take their horses, stabled at a tavern further down Bread Street. Instead they would walk, for in some places the snow was knee-deep. The whole city looked as if it was under a carpet of white damask; underfoot the snow was frozen hard, while the ice, in huge jagged icicles, hung like tear-drops from the intricate gabled tiers of the houses. They turned into Cheapside. The busy thoroughfare, usually filled with stalls and shops, was deserted. The huge-framed merchant houses, built of strong thick oak and folded in with plaster three to four stories high, were all shuttered and covered in white except for those which bore the arms of the city shields of bright vermilion with a figure of St Paul in gold, the head, arms and feet of the saint in silver. The snow had slipped off these shields, making them blaze all the more fiercely against the whiteness. A friar, ghost-like, hurried by; his white robe would have made him blend with the snow but for the exquisite cope he wore round his shoulders which concealed the viaticum he carried to some sick person. Two tired boys, desperately attempting to keep their candles alight, preceded him.

To the left of Corbett, towering above the city, the huge sombre mass of St Paul's, snow still packed on its vaulted dome, made the clerk concentrate on his problems until, near exhausted by the snow, they reached the Shambles. Here carts took the offal, fat and other refuse from the butchers to be dumped in the Fleet River. One or two cartloads had already departed, leaving pools of red blood, and not even the snow could hide the terrible stench of the place. Faces turned against the biting wind, they passed the now open, double-barred gates of Newgate. Ranulf ceased his cursing for here, in the buildings around the gate, was the terrible prison where he had spent a night preparing to be hanged at Tyburn so many years ago. He felt his anger against Corbett ebb and, putting his head down to shield his face against the biting wind, he plodded on behind his master, wondering how long this terrible journey would last. They passed through the city gates; on the right the huge ditch, six feet deep and, in some places, seven yards wide, where the refuse of the city was dumped. In the summer, it would reek to high heaven but now, packed with ice, it served as a play area for a number of boys who, with shinbones fastened to their feet, were busy skating onto the ice. Beneath its frozen surface, Ranulf could see the corpses of dogs and cats and, he was sure, the perfectly formed body of a child.

Corbett and Ranulf moved across the open fields of Smithfield, past the charred execution block and towards the lofty pointed archway of St Bartholomew's hospital. The gate was open so they went in, following the immense walls; stables, smithies and other storehouses. The hospital itself, a long and huge hall, was approached by a flight of steps. Here, Corbett stopped a lay brother and asked to see Father Thomas. The old man nodded, gave a gap-toothed smile, the saliva drooling out from one corner of his mouth, and shuffled away. They waited at the top of the steps. Corbett could smell crushed herbs, spices and other substances he could not name. At last, a lanky, stooping figure came out of the doorway, hands extended, his face wreathed in smiles when he saw Corbett.

'Hugh, it is good to see you.' He put his arms round the clerk's shoulder, towering above him, as he gave Corbett a vice-like hug.

'Father Thomas,' Corbett said, 'may I introduce my servant and comrade,' he added caustically, 'Ranulf-atte-Newgate.'

Father Thomas bowed, his thin, narrow, horse-like face now solemn and courteous as if Corbett had just introduced him to the King of England. Father Thomas and Hugh had known each other since their student days at Oxford. The clerk had always admired this tall, ugly man with his friendly eyes and ever-smiling mouth. He had studied abroad in the hospitals of Paris and Salerno, and his knowledge of drugs and herbs could not be equalled.

Father Thomas ushered them into the long hall. It was clean and well swept; thick woollen coverings decorated the walls; the windows were boarded up with shutters and over these, to soften the austere look of the place, large multi-coloured drapes had been hung. On either side of the hall was a row of beds; beside each a stool, and at the foot a small leather trunk. Lay brothers and other priests moved quietly from bed to bed administering what remedies they could. Corbett believed most doctors did not relieve sickness, but at least, here, the brothers of St Bartholomew's made death comfortable and afforded it some dignity. Father Thomas led them through the hall to a small, white-washed chamber beyond, sparsely furnished with two tables, a bench, a few stools and a chafing-dish to warm the room. Along the walls were shelves filled with pots of crushed herbs, their fragrant smells even more delightful on such a cold wintry morning. Father Thomas made them sit, serving them mulled wine in wooden beakers. Ranulf found the wine hard to keep down although he was grateful for the hot spicy liquid. Once they were comfortable, Father Thomas went behind the table and, sitting down, leaned over, his face creased with concern.

'So, Hugh? Why do you wish to see me? Are you well?'

'I want to talk about poisons, Father Thomas,' Corbett replied, enjoying the shocked look in the priest's eyes.

He leaned over and tapped the priest's long bony fingers. 'Come now, Father,' he said, 'I am not here to make any confession. Nor do I normally discuss poisons, but tell me about the various types.'

Father Thomas grimaced and haltingly gave a list of poisons, the drugs from plants such as belladonna and foxglove. As he warmed to his subject, he provided detailed descriptions of each poison: how they were made; how they were to be administered; their side effects and possible antidotes. As he spoke, Ranulf, who found most of the terms difficult to understand, realized one thing: his secretive master believed the priest who had collapsed in St Paul's the previous day had been poisoned; he also understood that whoever had administered the poison had done so during the sacrifice of the mass, for all the deadly poisons Father Thomas described acted within minutes.

At last Father Thomas finished and Hugh nodded.

'You probably know why I have come?' Father Thomas shook his head and spread his hands.

'Here we have our own tasks, Hugh. I hear very little of what is going on,' he grinned, 'except your promotions. It's a long time, Hugh, since we were at college together. Oxford seems so far away. Strange,' he looked through the narrow-slitted window at the icy fields beyond, 'when you look back, how everything seems to have taken place at the height of summer? Do you know, I can never remember studying during the winter or when it was cold? The sun always seemed to shine.'

Hugh smiled, he quietly agreed. Whenever he thought back to his days at Oxford, or to his marriage to Mary, each day, each memory was always against a background of summer, of warm suns, lush green grass, trees moving gently in a soft breeze; the chatter of his little girl, the serene influence of his wife. Perhaps that was what the memories were for: to warm, bolster and strengthen you for the future.

Corbett shrugged, rose and, extending both hands towards Father Thomas, cupped the man's head in his hands, kissing him gently on the brow.

'Father Thomas,' he said, 'believe me. The paths I walk now, even though bounded by a wickedness you could not even comprehend, are made easier because of my friendship with you and the memories we share.'

Father Thomas rose, clasped Hugh's hand and, mildly protesting that the clerk did not come to see him often enough, led them back to the main gateway of the hospital.

Corbett, followed by a now grumbling Ranulf, began the long walk across Smithfield, back through Newgate. By now the city had come to life; booths were open and shop fronts, overhung with canvas to protect them against the inclement weather, were let down. A line of prisoners being taken from Newgate down to the King's Bench at Westminster passed them; they were shackled together with iron gyves around their ankles, wrists and necks, and made to trot through the snow. Some of them, young boys and girls, had no shoes or leg coverings and their cries were piteous as they scarred their feet on the hard ice and the rocky filth hidden beneath. A group of bawds, hauled in by the city bailiffs for walking the streets the previous evening, was being taken into the prison; their scarlet gowns and hoods were ripped and torn and white hats had been placed on their heads. A solitary bagpiper preceded them, whilst alongside shambled files of tired-looking soldiers who returned the obscene jokes or jests of the women with the occasional slap or coarsened oath. A beggar rushed out to Corbett, one eye missing, her nostrils eaten away by some terrible disease; she had a mewling infant clasped tightly to her breast.

'*Ayez pitié! Ayez pitié!*'

Corbett stopped. The woman knew Norman French. Once she may have been a lady, someone of quality, a discarded mistress who had begun to fall from the ranks of the city's caste system and was now at the bottom, here in the sewers and shambles of Newgate and the Fleet.

'*Ayez pitié!*' she repeated.

Corbett dug into his purse and handed over two silver coins. The woman smiled and turned away. As she did so, Corbett realized the bundle she carried was not an infant but a small cat. The woman was a professional beggar; she had disguised her face with horrific sores and presented herself as a true object of pity.

Corbett smiled wryly at Ranulf. 'Isn't it strange? Even when you want to show compassion, things go wrong.'

Ranulf shrugged, he did not understand his master, nor his fitful gesture of generosity; they seemed ill-placed for a man who, only a few hours earlier, had dragged him from his bed and thrown him into the ice-cold snow. They walked on, turning left to go down Old Dean's Lane and into Bowyer's Row, south along Fleet Street, past the ditch, its filth frozen in ice, then passing White Friars, the Temple, Gray's Inn and the rich, timbered gilt-edged houses of the lawyers, before joining the main thoroughfare to the palace and abbey of Westminster.

Scenes of frenetic business greeted them: lawyers in striped hoods, judges in their red, ermine-lined gowns, preceded by tipstaffs, bailiffs, officials and the occasional knight banneret of the royal household. All carried themselves with that hurried air of importance with which notables endow themselves to emphasize their rank and make the exercise of their own authority so much easier.

Corbett and Ranulf jostled their way through them, past the Clock Tower and up the broad, sweeping staircase into the main hall of Westminster. Corbett had been here many times. Usually his work was in the Chancery offices of the king's chamber which were situated wherever the king decided to hold court: sometimes south of the river at Eltham, or the Tower or the Palace of Sheen, or one of the royal manors in a distant shire. But always they came back to Westminster. Here, in the alcoves of the great hall, were the different courts, the exchequer, the Common Pleas and, on the dais, the King's Bench, where the Chief Justice, aided by other royal judges, dispensed justice in the king's name. Leading off from the hall were a warren of passageways, small chambers and offices: the royal messengers, the king's comptrollers and conveyors, the surveyor of works, the controller of the royal household, the chamberlain; each had their own little empire.

Corbett was pleased to be temporarily free of the bureaucratic politics which dominated each and everyone who worked here, for, as chief clerk to the Chancery, he was moved around from one department to another. Usually he was present when the king sealed charters with the Great Seal of England, with other barons present being there to ratify the document. On a few occasions only he and the king were present as letters were despatched under the Secret or Privy Seal to officials, sheriffs, bailiffs or Commissioners of Array in the shires. Corbett enjoyed his work. He liked writing, the study of manuscripts, the preparation of vellum, the joy of inscribing a fresh, pumice-rubbed piece of high quality parchment, the smell of the dried ink and sharpened quills. There was excitement when letters were brought in to be transcribed and satisfaction in seeing suitable replies despatched.

Now, for the third or fourth time, the king had asked him to take up special duties. Corbett, if he was honest with himself, would admit he was frightened. His previous tasks had taken him abroad and pitted him against powerful figures in shadowy, lawless areas of London. He had faced charges of treason in Wales and Scotland as well as murderous attempts on his life. Corbett had few illusions: he knew it was only a matter of time before either he failed disastrously and incurred the royal wrath of Edward or suffered some serious accident. Then what? The king might well discard him like one would an old rag or a useless piece of parchment, to be swept away like the leaves of the previous summer to be forgotten and not counted. And who would miss him? In his own way he loved Ranulf but he also had no illusions about his servant. There was only Maeve in Wales. Corbett stopped and squinted up at one of the great bay windows of the hall. It was now the middle of January and the last time he had seen her was the previous autumn. The lapse of time only increased his aching longing for her. If he thought about Maeve's serene face and long blonde hair, her perfect rounded figure, any feeling of pleasure would be replaced by a deep black depression. He knew he could not go to Wales and the weather made it impossible for her to travel to London. He would have to see this matter through and take what came.

Perhaps that was why he was frightened; he wanted to live now more than he ever did before. He was frightened of dying, of something happening which would stop him meeting Maeve, prevent them from being married and living as man and wife. For if he died what then? What use the tenements in Bread Street or Aldermanbury, or his other possessions – the little brown padlocked chest in the goldsmith's house in Cheapside or the empty, derelict manor in Sussex? What good would all these do if his body was rotting away in some pauper's grave or in some lonely London ditch?

Corbett pulled back his cloak and, without thinking, touched the long dagger which swung from his belt. Immediately he was accosted by an important official dressed in scarlet and blue doublet and hose, with his hair neatly coiffed. He carried a white wand of office which marked him as a Steward of the Great Hall. He placed his hand on Corbett's chest as a gesture he should go on further. The man's self-important face beamed with pleasure at being able to exercise power and his chest puffed out like some little cock-sparrow. In other circumstances Corbett would have laughed but now he glared into the man's pig-like face.

'You stop me, sir?'

'I stop you, sir,' the pompous fool replied, 'because you are armed, here near The King's Bench and that is an offence!' He clicked his fingers at a watching group of men-at-arms to come and arrest Corbett when suddenly, the clerk brought both hands firmly down on the man's shoulder with a resounding thwack.

'What is your name?'

The official's eyes became guarded. Corbett was not drunk nor did he seem deranged; only a man sure of himself would make such a gesture in the face of royal authority.

'What is your name?' Corbett repeated sternly.

'Edmund de Nockle,' the pompous idiot replied.

'Well Edmund,' Corbett said, pressing his hands deeper into the man's shoulders until he saw the fellow wince, 'my name is Hugh Corbett. I am senior clerk in the king's Chancery, a special emissary in matters of the secret seal. Now, if you wish me arrested that is your privilege, but I assure you before the day is out, I will be back in this hall wearing my sword and dagger and you, you arrogant fool, will be shackled in the Marshalsea Prison.'

The man was about to apologize but Corbett would not

let him go. 'Now, Master de Nockle. You will lead us to where the king is.'

The man, pink-faced with embarrassment, chose to ignore Ranulf's snigger and, turning smartly on his heel, led them out of the hall, down some stairs and along a winding corridor. Corbett knew full well where the king was. The royal chamber was off the writing-room near where the letters and seals were kept. De Nockle approached a huge, iron-barred door and knocked gently, but Corbett, deciding that he had had enough, pushed him aside and rapped more loudly. He heard the king's voice calling entry so he opened the door and went in with Ranulf close behind.

7

The king was at the far end of the room, sitting on a huge chest. Around him the floor was covered with rolls of parchment and vellum; a roaring fire burnt in the chimney and the hearth around was littered with bits of coal and wood. Corbett felt the intense heat immediately, for the windows were all shuttered and the room contained at least three braziers as well as the fire. The clerks working at the long table looked as if they regretted putting on so many layers of clothing. The king was dictating letters, now and again breaking off to start another, so all four scribes were virtually writing at once. Corbett had seen the king work like this, an amazing spectacle as he moved from one item to another: whether it be a letter to a sheriff ordering him to be more prompt and accurate in producing the profits of a shire, or to a cardinal in Rome asking him to plead a certain matter with His Holiness.

On Corbett's entry, Edward rose and immediately barked at the scribes to leave. He did not have to repeat his commands. They dropped their pens and filed gratefully from the room. Edward filled two large cups of wine to the brim and brought them over to Corbett and Ranulf. He heard his servant splutter his thanks and noisily guzzle the wine. Edward always surprised Corbett. Sometimes he could be arrogant but then again he could remember the smallest detail about a servant, even going on an errand personally to make matters more comfortable for a menial of the household.

Today, the king was apparently in such a mood. He waved both Corbett and Ranulf to a bench.

'You have been out early, Master Clerk?' The king laughed at the surprised look in Corbett's eyes. 'I sent a messenger to your lodgings and was told you had gone. You have begun to investigate the matter in St Paul's?'

'I have, Your Grace.'

'And what have you found?'

'Nothing much.' Corbett saw the King's eyes darken and realized how fickle the man was. 'I mean, Your Grace, I have learnt a little more. De Montfort was definitely poisoned but the venom used must have been administered during the sacrifice of the mass, probably during the communion of the celebrants. He died within a few minutes of taking the poison.'

'Do you know who administered it?'

'It could be anyone, Your Grace. The finger even points at you.'

The king came so close to Corbett that the clerk could smell the mixture of royal sweat and rare perfume. 'What do you mean, Clerk?'

'Your Grace, you did send wine to de Montfort the evening before the mass was celebrated.'

'I did,' the king replied guardedly.

'You sent it with Fulk Bassett?'

'Yes, that is true,' the king repeated quickly, watching Corbett carefully and casting sidelong glances at Ranulf as if he now regretted his generosity and would like to order the servant from the room. Ranulf needed no second bidding. Putting the cup down, he sprang to his feet, bowed to the king and backed gracefully out of the chamber muttering how he had forgotten something in the great hall. He would have to hasten back and if His Grace and Master Corbett would excuse him then his voice trailed off. Ranulf opened the door and fled down the corridor, leaving his master to face the royal wrath. Corbett waited until he was gone, before speaking.

'Your Grace, the wine you sent was poisoned with the same venom that killed de Montfort. I don't know the precise combination, arsenic, belladonna, the juice of the foxglove, maybe all three. The same poison de Montfort drank during the mass was found in the pannikin of wine you sent him.'

'Do you think, Master Clerk,' the king replied, 'that I would poison wine?'

'No, I do not. But someone else poisoned it to make it look as if you did. Who knows, even Bassett himself.'

The king shook his head. 'Bassett would do nothing, not even draw breath, without the royal command,' he said drily. 'But do you believe all this, Corbett?'

'No, your Grace, I do not.'

'Why?'

'The poison given to de Montfort was a powerful one. As I have said, he died within a few minutes. The wine you sent was opened the evening beforehand.'

'He could have drunk it before the mass?'

'No, he could not, Your Grace; you forget your Canon Law. No one who receives communion or celebrates mass must eat or drink after midnight.'

The king shrugged. He knew some of these priests, they made burdens for other men's backs which they never carried themselves.

'Still, Your Grace,' Corbett persisted, 'even if he had drunk it, he would never have reached the altar alive.'

The king nodded. 'So it would look as if someone,' Edward squinted up at the light streaming through one of the shutters – 'It looks as if somebody wanted to kill de Montfort and make it look as if I wanted to kill him. At the same time, you say, I could have been the intended victim. Perhaps there is no solution.'

'There will be, Your Grace,' Corbett replied confidently. 'If a problem exists, a solution must exist. We must find out who administered the poison or when it was administered. The answer to either of these questions will lead us to the truth.'

The king went back and sat on the bench, his legs apart, head in hands. He rubbed his face, a favourite gesture, toyed with one of the many precious rings on his fingers and looked up at Corbett.

'I know you, Clerk. You have not come here to tell me the obvious. You have come here to ask something haven't you?'

'Yes, Your Grace.'

'Then for God's sake,' the king bellowed, 'ask it!'

Corbett took a deep breath.

'I don't think anyone would believe, Your Grace, the wine you sent to de Montfort was poisoned by you, but they might ask why you sent the wine in the first place.'

The king shrugged. 'A gift, a peace offering.'

Corbett rose, picked up a stool and walked over to sit close to the king. 'Your Grace, you know I am your obedient servant.' Edward looked at him warily. 'Your Grace,' Corbett repeated, 'I *am* your obedient servant, but if you wish to find out the truth then, with all respect, I must urge you to tell me the truth. You hated the de Montfort family. You hated the Dean of St Paul's. He was going to denounce you and your taxes before the entire English Church. His words would have gone abroad to the Pope in Avignon, to King Philip in Paris, to the Archbishops and Bishops of Scotland and Wales. So why did you send him the wine?' Corbett licked his lips. 'It could not be a bribe, not to a man like de Montfort. You would need the wealth of an abbey to buy a man like that.'

The king smiled. 'You have a sharp brain, Master Corbett. Sometimes too sharp.' The king rose and walked restlessly round the room. 'But you are wrong. De Montfort was not going to denounce me. In fact, I had bribed him already. I had bought him, Master Clerk. In his speech after mass he was not going to attack the Crown's claims on the Church's revenues but support them.' The king paused to watch Corbett's astonishment. 'You see,

Master Clerk, you are probably an honest man. In your own lights an incorruptible one. You make the mistake of thinking that because you do something or think something, other people do the same. But they do not.' The king jangled the purse which swung from the gold, jewel-encrusted belt lashed round his waist. 'Silver and gold, Master Corbett. I bought de Montfort. A mixture of bribes and threats.'

'And the wine?'

'The wine was sent, Master Corbett, as a gesture to seal our understanding. De Montfort liked the luxuries of the world. Your investigations will prove my suspicions correct. You see, Corbett, yesterday, I was not angry about de Montfort's death but I was angry that he had not at least lived to deliver the sermon I had bought. I virtually wrote it for him myself – chapter and verse. It went back in history: how the Church in this country had constantly supported the monarchs. How Erconwald himself, Bishop of London, the great Saxon by whose tomb I stood yesterday, had done so much for the city, the king and the kingdom.

'I am still angry de Montfort is dead, and I need to find the assassins. Did they kill him for some private reason, or did they kill him because they knew he had been bought? Body and soul de Montfort was mine. His killer is my enemy and I suspect sits close, even at the right hand, of that pompous treacherous prig, Robert Winchelsea, Archbishop of Canterbury.'

The king's chest heaved and Corbett noted that Edward was on the verge of one of his notorious royal rages. The king smacked his hands together and his pacing became more vigorous.

'I can tolerate bishops who oppose me for the right reasons, Master Clerk, but not Winchelsea! He has sly conniving ways, scurrying to Rome, to Avignon, appearing to be a saint, a Becket in finer clothes. Winchelsea is a politician who plots against me. He would like me to be beholden to him. He sees himself as a defender of the Church's liberties. I suspect,' the king almost spat the words out, 'he would relish the fate of Becket and, if he is not careful, he may well meet it.'

Corbett shrugged. The king, watching him closely, returned to sit on the trunk facing him, his anger apparently forgotten.

'You seem surprised, Master Clerk.'

'I am surprised, Your Grace,' Corbett replied. 'Because if I accept what you say, I must also accept the premise that someone discovered that de Montfort had been bought and then killed him. I still believe, however, that whoever murdered de Montfort wished to strike at you.'

'But they have done just that,' the king replied. 'They have stopped de Montfort speaking on my behalf and yet,' the king laughed falsely, 'they have made it appear I was responsible for his death. A clever move, Master Corbett. A brilliant stratgem.'

Corbett shook his head. 'I believe it is worse than that. There is an assassin in this city, Your Grace, who wants you dead. De Montfort was simply a means to an end. I actually believe,' Corbett continued, 'that something went wrong with the plot. One day I hope to prove it.'

The king leaned forward and virtually jabbed his finger in Corbett's face. 'Give me one shred of proof for this.'

'There is one shred of proof. The wine you sent. Why should someone make the clumsy mistake of poisoning it? After all, with de Montfort dead and no speech, why poison the wine? A matter known only to me and one of the canons of St Paul's.' Corbett chewed his lip. 'You see, Your Grace, the murderer, the assassin, made a fatal error. He panicked, for the wine was poisoned not before de Montfort's death but afterwards, to make it look as if you were responsible.'

The king rubbed his face and Corbett waited for him to speak.

'Well, well, Master Clerk,' he finally concluded. 'If you

still have your doubts, you had better continue with this matter.'

'I will, Your Grace, on one condition.' The king looked sharply at him. 'On the one condition,' Corbett repeated firmly, 'that you tell me now whatever information you have about de Montfort. If I had known yesterday what you told me today it may have made my task easier.'

The king rose and walked across the room to peer through a crack in one of the shutters. Outside, the beautiful rose gardens of Westminster were carpeted in thick white snow. Nothing grew, no plants, no grass. He was tired of this interview. He feared men like Corbett, men from nowhere, with brains as sharp as the finest razors, a man who could not be bought. Edward knew, deep in his heart, that if Corbett was ever given a task which went against his conscience, the clerk would not do it. If Corbett found a matter which should be rectified, irrespective of the royal wishes, Edward suspected that Corbett would see it as a matter of conscience to do so. The king respected Corbett but saw him as a prig and slightly self-righteous. Edward sighed. He did not really care who had killed the pathetic de Montfort, a base-born, mercenary priest! Edward knew such men could be bought with anything, a house, gold, promotion to high office. What he really wanted was to find out who had spoiled his plan to embarrass Winchelsea. The king felt the rage still seething within him. Oh, how he would have loved to have listened to de Montfort's speech and quietly relished the stupefaction on Winchelsea's face and those of his sanctimonious fellow bishops! The king wanted that. And, above all, he needed the money the Church had in its bulging coffers to launch fresh raids across the Scottish march; to equip a new fleet and take it to Flanders; send his armies across France's northern borders; teach Philip of France a sharp, hard lesson of how English lands there were best left alone. It might still be possible. Perhaps Corbett would achieve this or, at least, help to achieve it. The king turned and smiled at Corbett.

'Master Clerk, I can tell you nothing more. You have our full assurance that whatever you do to unearth the terrible murderer and blasphemer will be supported by us, however long it takes.'

Corbett, recognizing the sign for dismissal, rose, bowed and backed out of the room. In the passageway he gave a deep sigh, grateful the meeting was over. He was fully aware Edward did not really like him but Corbett was equally determined to show the king that he did not trust him. He heard a door open and spun round. The king stood there still smiling like some indulgent father.

'Master Corbett,' he called out, 'your betrothed in Wales, Maeve ap Morgan?'

Corbett nodded.

'If this matter is resolved, we will let you leave our service so you can visit her.' The king continued to smile. 'Indeed, if it is resolved quickly, we will ensure she is brought here to London, to our court. Of course, if you fail,' the king bit his lip as if reluctant to continue. 'But,' he added ominously, 'we are sure you will not fail us.'

Corbett again bowed. When the door was closed he spun on his heel and strode down the corridor, aware of both the royal promise as well as the silent threat.

Corbett spent the rest of the day in his own writing-room, drawing up warrants in the king's name, which declared that Hugh Corbett, clerk, had the royal authority to act on certain matters, and all sheriffs, bailiffs, officials and everyone who owed allegiance to the king, should give him assistance in his task. Once these letters had been drafted and written by Corbett's chief assistant, a small, mouse-like man, William Hervey, they were sent for the king's approval and sealing. Corbett then finished other minor matters, gave orders to his subordinates, sent a servant to seek out Ranulf and instructed Hervey to meet him outside the great door of St Paul's shortly after prime the following morning. The little man nodded his head vigorously; he liked Corbett, who protected and entrusted him with special tasks. At the same time he was in awe of the senior clerk's evident ease of access to the king and other great lords. For his part, Corbett trusted Hervey completely. The man hardly lived outside the Chancery offices, his fingers constantly stained with the grease waxes and different coloured inks they used. He had virtually no life outside his calling; time and again, Corbett had to arouse him from sleep and send him home to his lonely dwellings in Candlewick Street.

Once all these matters were finished, Corbett met Ranulf in the great hall, now emptying of its officials, judges and lawyers. They went back up towards Bread Street where they stopped at a pastry shop, Corbett buying pies to eat as they walked, hot freshly cooked rabbit, diced and sprinkled with strong herbs. Both relished the meal as they hurried along, allowing the hot juices to run down their chins. At the corner of Bread Street Corbett took Ranulf into a tavern they frequented for their evening meal, usually a dish of stewed meat and vegetables, and tonight was no different. Ranulf, once he had drunk and eaten his fill though careful to avoid the excesses of the previous day, wandered off on his usual task of attempting to seduce someone else's wife or betrothed, leaving Corbett staring once again into the darkness.

Ranulf would have given half the gold he owned to know what the clerk was thinking and yet, if he had, it would have been money wasted, for Corbett just sat thinking about what the king had said, planning to-morrow's meeting, hoping that Hervey would ensure the canons Corbett had listed in his letter would be present in the chapter-house. Having gone over in his mind to satisfy himself all was well, Corbett once more turned to the matter of Maeve. So engrossed was he with his own private thoughts that he did not even notice the dark, cowled figure in the far corner glaring balefully across at him.

8

It did not snow that night and the outlaws were at least grateful for this small mercy as they stepped out of the line of trees, which marked the edge of Epping Forest, and made their way along the ice-covered track. Here the snow was not deep, having been scattered and crushed by the occasional cart and carriage which had braved the weather. They moved silently, six in number, all armed to the teeth. They wore an assortment of clothes: heavy leather jerkins over soiled lace shirts stolen from their victims or taken from a house they had ransacked; thick, woollen hose pushed into high leather boots; and cloaks of various colours wrapped tightly around their bodies. Each carried a number of daggers as well as swords in their broad leather belts and their leader, Robert Fitzwarren, boasted a small round shield and a conical steel helmet. He had had these ever since the day, years earlier when he had absconded from the royal commissioners of array, who had wanted to take him into Scotland with the king's armies. Fitzwarren had other ideas. He had killed the leader of his troop, stolen what money the fellow carried and, taking whatever arms were available, fled to the dark sanctuary of Epping Forest.

He had lived as an outlaw for years, turning felony into a successful business. The area was full of wolfs-heads, lawless men, peasants who had fled from their masters, soldiers who had deserted from the wars, criminals from the city, murderers, perjurers, blasphemers. Fitzwarren became their leader. Of course, there had been the occasional losses, the ambush which had gone wrong, those betrayed in taverns or drinking houses by some wench who believed her lover had crossed her, but Fitzwarren always survived and attracted other men to him like the glowing flame of a candle draws in the moths.

Now, however, his band had shrunk to less than ten men. It was difficult to track down the venison and even more dangerous to attempt assaults on lonely farmsteads. The peasants had become wary of him, taking steps to guard their families and stock at night. During spring and summer when the traffic of the road increased, the pickings were always easier but, even here, the ferocity of Fitzwarren's reputation had spread far and wide. Few people travelled alone; they were always in convoys and usually escorted by at least three or four soldiers from some castle or fortified manor house. Lately, however, Fitzwarren's luck had improved. When he attacked any traveller, convoy or house, he could only take what he needed: foodstuffs, weapons, clothes as well as enjoy the bodies of female captives. He had lived like an animal, hand to mouth, but then he had met the priest and a new venture had begun. Fitzwarren had begun to collect treasures, and simply moved them into London for the priest to sell. It was a highly profitable relationship which Fitzwarren encouraged, using all his greed and cunning. And if he raised enough money, what then? Perhaps buy a pardon? Re-enter society? Join the fold he had so often attacked?

This morning, however, Fitzwarren was angry, furious enough to leave the forests and take five of his closest followers with him. They kept to the line of trees as long as they could but, if they wanted to approach Cathall Manor, near the village of Leighton, they would have to go out in the open. Hence, Fitzwarren's strict instructions that they be armed to the teeth, each man carrying an arbalest and a quiver of evil-looking crossbow bolts.

As they came to the crossroads, Fitzwarren took his men back into the trees, sending forward the youngest to ensure all was safe. The young man crept forward like a hunting fox, his ears straining for any sound, his eyes momentarily blinded by the snowy whiteness. He looked out for any flash of colour, anything which would warn him not to proceed further. Like the rest, he was frightened of Fitzwarren. Their leader never tolerated failure; anyone who crossed him or failed to carry out a task could expect little mercy. The young man already felt nervous to be out of the forest. He spent most of his days there, protected by its deep darkness and the lack of paths; it was easy for pursuers to get lost, to fall into some marsh or bog and be sucked down, vanish for ever. Fitzwarren, however, knew the secret pathways and kept to them, so the young men realized the mission this morning must be highly important for their leader to take them out of the forest and so far out into the open.

The outlaw edged forward; the crossroads were deserted; on either side, the rough track continued between the line of trees. He could see or detect nothing. He looked at the black, three-branched gibbet which stood there, stark against the light blue sky. Three bodies hung from it in chains, a special punishment for those found guilty not only of robbery but murder as well. The young man grinned, showing a yellow, blackening row of teeth. He had known all three men. They were once members of Fitzwarren's gang, but they had disobeyed orders so Fitzwarren had handed them over to the sheriff's bailiffs at Chelmsford and received the reward. The men had been taken out late in the previous summer and left to dangle there. The bodies had long since decomposed, the eyes plucked out by hungry crows; only the whitening bones stirred gently in their iron cages, rattling as if in protest at the presence of the man who had betrayed them. The young man, satisfied that all was safe, indicated with his hand and was soon joined by his leader and comrades.

The gang walked in single file along the edge of the forest, following the track to the brow of the hill, where they stopped. Fitzwarren looked down at the deserted manor house, its huge encircling wall and barred gates. He gazed around. No sign, no movement: the place was deserted as usual. The only sign of any habitation was faint plumes of smoke on the horizon which rose from the fires and cooking-pots of the surrounding villages. He waited a while; from here he had a crow's-eye view of the entire manor house: the main building with outhouses running parallel to it, forming a courtyard. Usually such a place would be full of activity, grooms, ostlers, blacksmiths, but now it was empty, for the priest liked it that way. Satisfied that there was no danger, Fitzwarren led his small group down the slope through the snow. They avoided the main gate and moved like dogs around the curtain wall till they came to a small postern gate. As usual, this was open. They slipped in. The yard was a muddy quagmire. Fitzwarren examined the tracks carefully but there was nothing out of the ordinary. The stables, byres and barns were all empty and the fire in the blacksmith's long dead. He looked up and there, on the second storey of the manor house, he saw a red coverlet stuffed through a slit window, the sign that it was safe to approach. They walked up to the main door and confidently knocked. Footsteps sounded in the hollow passageway and the door swung open; the steward, Thomas Bassingham, stood there, his small anxious face attempting an ingratiating smile. Behind him, wiping her plump hands on a white apron, stood his wife.

'You are welcome, Master Fitzwarren,' he stuttered.

Fitzwarren smiled and, brushing him aside, strode into the manor house along the main hall into the kitchen and buttery beyond. No fire had been lit, according to his orders, but at least the man had had the sense to place warming dishes around the room and put burning charcoal into a rusting brazier. Bassingham's wife, terrified of these rough-looking men, quietly served them with cold meats, cheeses and flagons of rather watery mildewed beer. The outlaws ate greedily, slurping their food, indicating with their hands when they wanted more. Once they were finished Fitzwarren, seated in the large, oaken chair at the top of his table, stretched, belched loudly and brought his hands crashing down on the table.

'Well, Master Bassingham,' he said. 'You have news of your master?' The steward seemed exhausted. Fitzwarren peered closer. He noticed the lines of anxiety, the dark rings round his eyes, the unshaven face.

'Something has gone wrong?' he asked ominously.

Bassingham nodded. 'I came back from the city as fast as I could,' he bleated. 'I have been travelling ever since. The roads there are almost impassable. My horse –'

'Your horse?' Fitzwarren asked.

'I have not stabled it here,' the man replied smoothly. 'It is elsewhere. I finished the journey by foot. The snow, it is so deep. My wife, she thought I was dead.'

'She may well wish that you were if the news you have brought is not satisfactory.'

'It is not my fault,' the steward almost screeched. 'It's not my fault that the priest is dead.'

Fitzwarren shot to his feet. Bassingham recoiled at the malice in the outlaw's eyes.

'He what!'

'The priest is dead. He collapsed during the mass.'

'So you have brought nothing?'

'How could I? How could I? His house in London has been sealed. There are royal guards around it. The king himself is angry at de Montfort's death. What could I do?' the man whined.

Fitzwarren strode down the table and, grabbing the man by the front of his dirty jerkin, lifted him off his feet.

'You could have brought the gold that your master owes me.' Fitzwarren smiled evilly, his eyes gleaming.

'I could not bring it,' Bassingham replied anxiously, now

wishing he had not returned here. He should have stayed in London, fled. He looked sideways. Only his wife, fresh-faced, black curly hair, his beautiful Katherine, she would have pined away without him. Fitzwarren followed the steward's eyes and grinned.

'My men,' he said, 'my men have been in the forest long. It is wrong of me to give them nothing.' He turned and grinned over his shoulder at his comrades slouched round the table. 'Tie this rogue up and then,' he tossed Bassingham aside like a rag doll and walked over to the table, knocking off the dishes and cups with a sweep of his arm, 'and then he shall watch us have our pleasure.'

Bassingham screamed as the outlaws seized his wife but, as Fitzwarren knew, the manor house was deserted, the countryside lay under a heavy cloak of snow. Who could possibly come to their rescue? And Fitzwarren, the rage seething in him, felt that someone should pay for the terrible misfortunes he had suffered.

* * *

In London Corbett and Ranulf were attending a meeting of a totally different nature. Hervey had met them outside the south door of St Paul's and, together, they had entered the cathedral just as prime was finishing. Corbett gestured they should stay in the nave, which was still cloaked in darkness. He stared into the pool of light thrown by the tiers of candles which stood in their silver candelabra between the choir stalls. The canons there were now on the final psalm. Corbett listened carefully, letting his mind be soothed by the rise and fall of the chant: how the Lord was going to come on his day of judgement and bring justice to all nations. Corbett smiled wryly when he heard it. If the Lord was coming, he would spend most of his time dispensing justice here in St Paul's. Eventually the leading cantor began the Doxology: *Gloria Patri et Filio et Spiritui*

Sancto – the response being taken up in one triumphant chant. Silence fell, the canons filed out, candles were extinguished and darkness once more clothed the cathedral.

Corbett did not care if he had been seen or not but, after a brief wait, led Ranulf and Hervey up to the top of the nave, past the choir and out across the courtyard to the chapter-house. It was a different place from where the feast had been held only two days previously. The carpets had been rolled back, the tables stacked against the wall. At the top, on the dais, a group of cowled figures awaited him, their faces looking grotesque in the flickering candlelight, for dawn had not yet fully broken and the chapter-house was still dark and sombre. Corbett gazed around as he walked across the wooden floor, looking up at the shields which hung there, emblazoned with the arms of canons who had served the Church over the centuries: the different colours, blue, red, gold, sable, and the animals, lions, leopards couchant and passant, griffins, dragons, wyverns. Why, he wondered rather aimlessly, did men of God need such triumphant armorial bearings?

When Corbett reached the top of the hall, he bowed and stepped on to the dais. He walked to the head of the table, gratified to see the canons paying him the deference due to a messenger from the king. He lowered himself into the deep, oak-carved chair and gestured Ranulf and Hervey to sit on the bench alongside him. He counted, yes he was pleased, five canons, the same number as had concelebrated that fatal mass with de Montfort only two days ago. He studied them, recognizing Plumpton's fleshy face, acknowledging his supercilious glance with a nod. The rest were a mixed sort, young and old, some ascetic, others looking as if they have never fasted for an hour in their lives. All were dressed in dark robes, their cuffs and cowls lined with ermine. Each of them, however, wore the same wary, anxious look as if they dreaded what was going to happen next. Corbett glanced at them again, relishing the moment. For some strange reason he had an almost irrational hatred of these plump priests, these self-styled men of God, for he knew that one, maybe more, had been involved in murder, sacrilege and blasphemy. They sat there now in sanctimonious silence prepared to answer his questions and, if he put a foot wrong, protest loudly to their bishop, the Archbishop of Canterbury, the king, the pope or whoever would listen to them. Corbett allowed Hervey to unpack his writing trays and rolls of parchment. Ranulf sat, hands clasped together, fully enjoying the moment. To him it was like a sweet wine, to sit in judgement on his betters, especially if they were priests.

Once he saw Hervey was ready, Corbett began.

'Reverend Fathers, I am pleased you have acceded to my request, and that of His Grace the king, to meet me here in the chapter-house to discuss the events which occurred this week. Let me refresh your memories of the terrible event. A mass was held last Monday, celebrated by your dearly beloved colleague, Walter de Montfort, dean of this cathedral. Shortly before the communion the dean collapsed. His death was instantaneous. His body was taken to the sacristy and there given the last rites. I examined his corpse and I hasten to add,' Corbett lifted a hand, 'that though I am no physician, it is my belief he was poisoned. I also believe,' Corbett measured his words carefully, 'that the poison was administered during mass itself.' He heard the sharp intake of breath and mutters of "blasphemy". He again raised his hand. 'I put this to you merely as a theory. If anyone disbelieves it, let me tell you the facts as I know them.' Corbett then gave them the same description he had given the king. How de Montfort's rigid face, blackened mouth and tongue, as well as the suddenness of his death, were all symptoms of a fatal poisoning. He referred to Father Thomas, whom many of the canons must have known, and how the physician had informed him that all powerful poisons acted instantly. 'The question is,' Corbett concluded, 'who murdered him, and why?'

As expected, Sir Philip Plumpton was the first to answer.

'How do we know,' he jibed, 'especially since I have given you that flagon of wine, that our late lamented colleague, de Montfort, was not poisoned by the king, or,' he added, looking meaningfully at Corbett, 'by one of the king's minions?'

Corbett ignored the treasonable assertion. 'Again, I refer you to Father Thomas at St Bartholomew's,' he answered. 'He will tell you that if de Montfort drank the wine which the king sent, and which someone else undoubtedly poisoned, he would never have survived the opening prayers of the mass. Of course,' Corbett chose his words carefully to close the trap, 'if you are going to allege de Montfort drank wine and broke Canon Law by not fasting before he celebrated such a holy occasion, let those who saw him do so tell me now?'

His question was greeted with silent disapproval and a shuffling of feet.

'In which case,' Corbett continued crisply, 'perhaps we should proceed.' He nodded to where Hervey sat. 'This is Master William Hervey from the chancery office. He will transcribe my questions and your answers. So, sirs, your names and the offices held?'

Starting on Corbett's immediate left, each canon introduced himself.

'Sir John de Eveden, librarian,' – yellow-faced, thin, emaciated, with white tufts of hair springing out from his scalp. Corbett noticed the loose mouth and the shifty eyes which refused to meet his.

'David of Ettrick,' – the almoner, red-faced, small, completely bald, his podgy fingers fluttering in the air as he introduced himself and his office. Corbett detected a light Scottish ascent.

'Robert de Luce,' ascetic-looking, clean-shaven, his hair, hands and fingers carefully groomed, a studious man, well suited to his task of treasurer. 'Stephen Blaskett,' – young, fresh-faced, bright-eyed, his fingers marked with the same colours as those of Hervey. Corbett surmised, even before he spoke, that he must be chief clerk and secretary for the cathedral.

And finally, the fleshy-faced, charming Philip Plumpton, the sacristan. A man Corbett reckoned to be the most dangerous for, despite the smiling mouth, his eyes were agate-hard. A difficult man, Corbett thought a dangerous man to cross.

When the canons had finished introducing themselves, all of them showing deep resentment at his presence as well as his questions, Corbett took a piece of parchment and, pulling one of the silver candlebra closer to him, he drew an arc on the scrap of vellum.

'Let us say,' he began, 'this is the altar. Would you please indicate where you stood during the sacrifice of the mass.' After a great deal of careful questioning and ignoring Hervey's sighs of annoyance, Corbett had the order established. De Montfort would have been in the centre, on his far left Blaskett, then de Luce with Plumpton alongside the main celebrant, and on his right de Eveden and then Ettrick. 'Tell me,' Corbett continued, 'the order of the service.'

'You know it well,' Ettrick the almoner snapped. 'You were there. I saw you later, busy as a bee, going across our sanctuary.'

'You are from Scotland?' Corbett smiled at him.

'Yes, I am from Scotland,' the man replied. 'From just outside Edinburgh.' He leaned forward across the table and glared at Corbett. 'But before you utter it, I am a faithful subject of King Edward, as are many Scotsmen. Let me tell you that in his recent campaign against Berwick there were many Scots who fought on King Edward's side.'

'I am implying nothing,' Corbett answered soothingly. 'I simply asked if you were Scots. But help me refresh my memory, Master Ettrick. De Montfort would have stood at the centre of the altar facing the east, under the great rose window, above him the crucifix. Yes?'

Ettrick nodded.

'After the consecration, before the communion, what happened?'

Ettrick shrugged. 'We each had our paten, holding the consecrated host.'

'And you ate it?'

'Yes.'

'I do not wish to blaspheme,' Corbett said anticipating any shocked outburst, 'but are you sure that the hosts distributed after the consecration were not changed by anyone on the altar?'

'They couldn't have been,' the high-pitched voice of Blaskett intervened. 'Let us be honest: we were all at the altar. No deacon or server interferes with the bread or the wine after they have been transubstantiated.'

Corbett took careful notice of the theological terms the young man rather pompously used.

'But my question still stands, Sir Stephen,' he said. 'The hosts were consecrated and distributed for eating by whom?'

'By de Montfort.'

'No one else?'

'No one else,' Plumpton confirmed smilingly.

'And then what happened?'

'Oh, for the love of God,' de Eveden, the librarian, broke in quickly, 'you know what happened. Once the host was consumed, the wine was drunk.'

'Ah yes, the chalice. Who drank first?'

'De Montfort. He gave it to me and then,' the librarian paused, 'of course, to Ettrick, who brought it back to de Montfort. It was then passed to the celebrants on his left.'

'Who were?' Corbett interrupted.

'Plumpton, de Luce and Blaskett. That is right,' the librarian nodded. 'That was the order of the ceremony.'

Corbett held a finger up. 'The chalice was brought back?'

'Yes.'

'By whom?'

'By me.' Blaskett glared at Corbett.

'No, it wasn't!' De Luce, who had remained seated and watchful, now interrupted, his voice soft and mellow – a sharp contrast to the rest of the canons. 'Stephen, you did not bring it back.'

'Who did?' Corbett snapped.

'Why, Philip,' de Luce turned and stared at Plumpton opposite him, 'you gave it back to de Montfort.'

Plumpton's face grew angry. 'No, I did not. I ...' he paused and then slumped in his chair. 'Yes, you are right, Robert, I did. The chalice had been passed along de Montfort's left, I drank it, then you did, then Blaskett. Of course, Stephen,' Plumpton glared at him, 'you did not bring it back, I remember. You passed it along?'

Blaskett nodded. 'Yes, that it true.'

Corbett glanced at Hervey, whose pen was squeaking noisily across the parchment. 'Change your quill, Master Hervey.'

Hervey smiled gratefully for the respite, placed the hard pen down, picked up another, sharpened its point with a thin knife, dipped it in the inkpot, which he had warmed over one of the candles and began writing again.

'Now,' said Corbett, 'the chalice came back. What happened then?'

'We don't know,' de Luce continued softly. 'We had all eaten the host and drank the wine. What do you think we did, Clerk? We bowed our heads and said the usual words of thanksgiving.'

'Then what?' Corbett began to feel he was losing his grip on the meeting.

'I heard a sound,' de Luce continued. 'I looked up. De Montfort was turning, his hand was going towards his throat, the rest you know. He collapsed. By the time he was taken to the sacristy he was rigid in death.'

Corbett glanced round the table at the canons, their learned, worldly faces clear in the candle-light. He looked up at the stone-fitted window, noting that the room was becoming lighter. He felt frustrated. He resented the self-satisfaction of these five men. He had asked his questions and they had answered. There was nothing mysterious. What now, Master Clerk? they were silently taunting him. What can you ask now? Corbett thought of something.

'What if I told you,' he said slowly, 'that Sir Walter was to take the poisoned chalice to the king to drink before exchanging the kiss of peace with him?' Corbett relaxed, pleased at the hiss of intaken breath. 'What if,' Corbett looked up at the ceiling, 'I tell you that there are some who think that the chalice was not meant for de Montfort but for His Grace. May I remind you, sirs, that the murder, or even the attempted murder, of the Lord's Anointed is high treason. I need not remind you of the new penalties imposed for such a heinous crime. May I also remind you that there are some who maintain a poisoner should be boiled alive.' Corbett, very rarely vindictive, felt he wished to inflict some pain on these smug, self-satisfied men. 'I have heard of a man boiled alive in Wales. He was lashed to a pole and lowered, feet first, into a huge steaming cauldron. His screams lasted for half an hour as the flesh peeled away from his bones.'

Plumpton rose suddenly, rapping the table with his beringed hand. 'You have no right to frighten us, Clerk!' he said. 'You are insinuating that somebody here poisoned de Montfort but really intended to commit high treason and kill, King Edward. It is true, Clerk,' Plumpton continued remorselessly, 'that we may resent His Grace's demand for taxation, but to resent and argue is not treason. In fact, it is the Church's function to advise the king. The Church anointed Edward. No prince has received such loyalty from this cathedral as our present King Edward.'

He was about to continue but de Luce put his hand over his colleague's.

'Sit down, Philip,' Robert said, half smiling. 'I know what our visitor is saying. A dreadful crime,' he continued seriously, 'was committed. One of our brethren was murdered during the sacrifice of the mass, poisoned, if you are to believe Master Corbett. He has nothing to gain from this yet he implies the person who plotted de Montfort's death also plotted that of our king. These are, brethren, most serious and dreadful crimes.'

Corbett was grateful for de Luce's intervention, though he disliked intensely his calm demeanour, as if he was soothing children and included Corbett amongst them. There was a pause in the proceedings; Ettrick rose and went to a small table in the far corner bearing a tray and a jug of wine with cups. He filled these, placed one down near Corbett and gave the rest to each of his colleagues, totally ignoring the outraged expressions of Hervey and Ranulf. A dish of sweetmeats was also distributed. Corbett noticed with wry amusement how no one dared raise a cup or eat a sweetmeat. Ettrick sat down but, observing the silence around him, smiled, shrugged, got up again and came to where Corbett sat. He lifted the cup, toasted him and sipped carefully from it.

'Master Clerk, you may rest assured,' he said, 'that your wine is the best Bordeaux and contains no poison.' The half jest helped to relieve the tension. Corbett smiled, picked up the cup and drank, relishing the full-bodied taste. He passed the cup to Ranulf, indicating with his finger that the sweetmeat placed beside him was also his.

'Let us accept,' Corbett began, 'that de Montfort was murdered. Let us also accept that somebody close to him, who works in this cathedral, wanted him dead. How did they do this? And why?' Corbett narrowed his eyes. 'Why should they go to the trouble of poisoning wine after de Montfort was dead? For I am sure that's when the wine the king sent to de Montfort was poisoned. What did the assassin really intend? Who had grudges against de Montfort?'

This brought almost a giggle from de Eveden. Corbett turned.

'You find that amusing, Sir?'

'I find it amusing, Sir,' the librarian retorted sarcastically. 'You asked who had a grudge against de Montfort. I ask you, Sir Clerk, who did not?'

'What my brother is saying,' Plumpton interrupted, 'is that Master de Montfort was a powerful man, a lonely one; he was very disliked.'

'For what reason?'

Plumpton shrugged. 'He was vindictive, secretive. He never forgave a grudge. He always settled every grievance.' Plumpton looked around, wide-eyed. 'Why not let's tell the truth. Each of us here had a grievance.'

'That is not true!' Blaskett shouted back.

'You wouldn't have said that,' Plumpton added maliciously, 'if de Montfort had got into your bed!'

The young secretarius tried to stammer some reply but Corbett raised his hand to quell the argument.

'It will not serve,' he said, 'for us to argue. I take your point, Sir Philip. I have already gathered that Sir Walter was indeed a strange man and would have had many questions to answer. Perhaps it is best if I interview you each separately.' His invitation was greeted with a murmur of approval. 'Perhaps,' Corbett continued, 'I should begin with Sir John.'

The librarian bowed his assent and Corbett waited while the rest withdrew.

9

'Master de Eveden,' Corbett began. 'I am here on the king's business. Tell me, did you hate de Montfort?'

De Eveden paused before answering. 'Yes, I think I did.'

'Why?'

'He was arrogant.'

'In what matters?'

'In all matters,' the priest snapped. 'He exercised his authority. He liked to display his knowledge. He came constantly to the library demanding to know which manuscripts we held, where they were stored, how they were cared for.' De Eveden paused as if searching for words. 'There was something about the man. Something secretive, hypocritical.'

'You believe he was a hypocrite?'

De Eveden looked squarely at Corbett. 'Yes, I did.'

'Why do you say that?'

'At times, at night he went out by himself. No one knew where.'

'Was he the only priest who went out at night?' Corbett asked.

'No, he had visitors here. Oh, he kept them well away from us. There was a woman, whom he often met in the church. They would stand in the nave talking. It was always after vespers, when the place was deserted.'

Corbett thought of the woman he had seen on the day of de Montfort's death.

'Do you know who she is?'

'No. She was always richly caparisoned like some fat palfrey, silks and velvets. You could smell the stench of her perfume from the choir stalls.'

'You often sat there?'

'Yes, I did,' Eveden replied. 'I spied on de Montfort, if that is what you are saying. I hated the man.'

'Do you know the relationship between de Montfort and his strange woman visitor?' Corbett asked.

'No, I do not. I suspect she was his mistress.'

'But, Sir Philip Plumpton ...' Corbett said slowly, 'he insinuated that de Montfort was a sodomite and attempted to corrupt the young priest, Blaskett.'

De Eveden snorted with laughter.

'It wouldn't take much to corrupt Blaskett!'

'What does that mean?'

'Ask him yourself, Clerk. I am not here to answer questions about him.'

'Yes, that's right,' Corbett continued. 'You are here to answer questions about de Montfort. Tell me, in the days before de Montfort's death, did you have any argument with your dean?'

'No, I tried to avoid him.'

'On the day he died during the mass, you drank from the chalice and passed it back? Is that correct?'

'No,' de Eveden replied quickly. 'I did not. Remember, I was standing immediately on de Montfort's right. After me, Ettrick drank from the chalice before handing it to de Montfort who gave it to the other three. They touched and drank from it after I did.'

'Ah, yes,' Corbett said, 'when the chalice finally returned you were standing next to it, as you said, immediately on de Montfort's right.'

De Eveden smiled. 'You forget one thing, Clerk – de Montfort had already taken the chalice and drunk from it. He did not do so again.'

'How do you know that?'

The man seemed lost for words. 'That was the rite.'

'But you didn't actually see him not drink from it?'

'I didn't see him drink from it again,' de Eveden emphasized. 'Anyway, what are you saying? Do you think de Montfort would have just stood there and let me put some powder into the chalice and tell him to drink again? Wouldn't you think that was suspicious?'

'Yes, I would,' Corbett said. 'Thank you, Sir Priest.'

De Eveden glared at him, gave the sketchiest of bows, rose and stalked out.

Plumpton was next. He waddled in, his face wreathed in smiles. Corbett asked him the same questions and received the same answers. Yes, he hated de Montfort. Why? Because he believed de Montfort was the wrong man for such high office. He made the same insinuations against de Montfort's private life but offered no substantial evidence. Corbett nodded understandingly as he talked. Plumpton seemed satisfied with his answers and Corbett allowed him to run on until, just before the priest thought he was going to be dismissed, Corbett leaned forward and touched the man gently on his hand.

'Two problems concern me,' he said. 'You were standing to the left of de Montfort at the altar?'

'Yes, I was.'

'The chalice was passed back by you after the other celebrants had drunk from it?'

'That is correct.'

'It would have been easy, Sir Priest, to put some potion in?'

Plumpton shrugged. 'It would have been easy,' he agreed, 'except for two things. First, de Montfort did not trust me. He was sharp-eyed, and would have seen me put anything into the chalice. The mass would have stopped as dramatically as it did, only for a different reason. The second thing, Master Clerk, is that, as I am sure Sir John de Eveden has told you, de Montfort had already supped from the chalice. There was no reason for him to raise it to his lips again.'

Corbett sat and thought about what Plumpton had said. Had anyone seen Sir Walter raise the chalice again after it had been passed back? Yet, he must have drunk from it a second time just after the poison had been put in. For, if it had been there when he first drank from it, the other celebrants would also have died. So what did happen? He dismissed Plumpton courteously, but suddenly called him back.

'Sir Philip, I am sorry, there is one more question.'

The man turned, his hand on the latch of the door. 'What is it, Clerk?'

Corbett looked at him; he realized the priest's earlier friendship was a disguise; this man was dangerous, ambitious, ruthless. He took a slight insult as a serious threat, being a man who had probably risen, like himself, from common stock and believed every breath he drew should be fought for.

'Sir Philip,' Corbett said placatingly, 'I said there were two questions. The other one is this. You were very quick to point out that the wine sent by the king was poisoned. How did you know that?' Corbett watched the smile disappear from the man's face.

'I ...' he stammered.

'Yes, Sir Priest?'

'There is a small vestry off the sacristy. You may have noticed it. After we had brought the body in, I went in. The wineskin was lying there, the stopper on, the cup beside it. I uncorked it. It smelt strange. After you had examined de Montfort's corpse, so did I. I smelt the poison from de Montfort's rotten dead mouth, the same odour from the wine pannikin. I therefore concluded that someone had sent poisoned wine to de Montfort before the service began.'

'Did you put the wineskin there?'

'No, I did not.'

'What made you think that a priest who knew Canon Law would break his fast by drinking such wine?'

Plumpton shrugged. 'De Montfort broke many rules.'

'I have asked you that before. Which ones?'

'I don't know,' Plumpton cried. 'He was a very secretive man, very, very secretive. I am only the sacristan. Perhaps others can help you.'

'What made you think,' Corbett persisted, 'that it was de Montfort who drank from that bottle?'

'I didn't,' Plumpton retorted. 'I simply saw the wine pannikin, a cup beside it. I watched you examine de Montfort's body and sniff at his mouth. I followed suit, then went back and examined the pannikin. That was when I knew it was poison.'

'But you did not put it there?'

'No, I did not.'

'Then who did?'

'I don't know.'

'Thank you, Sir Priest.'

Once Plumpton had gone, Corbett turned to his two companions. Hervey, crouched over the parchment, was busy filling the white sheet with neat, blue-green letters. Ranulf just sat there, an astonished look on his face; for him the interrogation of such powerful priests was better than any miracle play or pageant seen in a London street. Corbett leaned over and with his fingers gently closed his servant's gaping mouth.

'Ranulf, I have never seen you so quiet.'

'Master,' Ranulf replied quickly, asserting himself, 'in the city, in the streets, we hear of these plump, rich priests. We see them walk like lords wherever they wish. They have their own courts, their own treasures. They live their own lives, have special rights and privileges.' He beamed at Corbett. 'I have never seen anyone interrogate them the way you have.'

Corbett smiled. 'Well, I am glad I have given someone pleasure.' He looked at Hervey but Hervey was lost to the world, fully immersed in what he was writing.

'Master William,' Corbett called. The little clerk looked

up. 'You are making a faithful copy?' The man nodded vigorously. 'Good. Ranulf, tell Master Ettrick we await him.'

Ranulf scrambled to his feet and disappeared out of the door. He returned immediately, the Scottish canon behind him, an aggressive look on his face. Even the way he walked seemed more suited to an army camp than to the precincts of a cathedral.

'Sit down, Master Ettrick.'

'Thank you.'

'You are Scots?'

'So I have said.'

'You have always been a priest?'

'No, I have not. I have often served the king in campaigns.'

'In whose retinue?'

'The Earl of Surrey's.'

'You are related to him?'

'No, I am not related to him!' Ettrick snapped back. 'But in King Edward's early wars in Scotland, I made myself useful to the king and, more particularly, to the earl.'

Corbett nodded. He knew what 'useful' meant; he had met such priests before in Scotland and Wales, men who had gone over to the side of the invader, supplying them with information, secret missives and rumours. A treacherous man? Corbett wondered. He would find out.

'And you received the prebend here?'

'I owe a great deal to the Earl of Surrey.'

'I am sure the earl trusts you as a faithful retainer?'

'He does.'

'But for the earl to obtain such a wealthy prebend,' Corbett continued, 'would also need the backing and support of the Bishop of London.'

'Not in this case,' the Scotsman replied. Corbett noticed how his accent became more pronounced as he fought to keep control of his temper.

'Then who?'

'I have only been a canon here for two years. I owe a debt of gratitude to his Lordship, Robert Winchelsea, the Archbishop of Canterbury.'

'Ah!' Corbett let out a sigh and stared up at the rafters.

'Is there anything wrong?' Ettrick asked bitingly. 'Is there anything wrong with my Lord Archbishop's recommendation?'

'No, Sir Priest, there is nothing wrong. Did you like de Montfort?'

Ettrick shrugged. 'As I have said, I have not been here very long, two years.'

'You have risen fast to the post of almoner. You are responsible for dispensing the cathedral's charity?'

'That is correct.'

'Therefore you must have had many dealings with the dean?'

'No, mainly with de Luce. I mean, Sir Robert de Luce.' Corbett noticed the change in the man's voice.

'He is the treasurer and I referred all matters to him.'

'Did you know anything about de Montfort?'

'Nothing. I very rarely talked to the man.'

'Why not?'

'I have no cause or grievance against him, I simply did not like him. I found him forbidding.'

'But you heard rumours?'

The Scotsman shrugged. 'In any community, the leader is disliked. Rumours, charges are levelled.'

'And what was said about de Montfort?' Corbett persisted with his questions.

The Scotsman gave a deep sigh. 'Nothing much. Nothing substantial. They just disliked the man, resented his leadership, his arrogance, his pride.'

'Did you find your new prebend suitable?'

'What do you mean?'

Corbett grimaced. 'For a Scotsman. England and Scotland are now at war.'

Ettrick bit back the reply. 'I have already told you,' he

said patiently, 'many Scotsmen's allegiance is to King Edward, not to some faction lord or robber baron, or that peasant Wallace.'

Corbett studied the man carefully. Now he saw real hatred in his eyes. This man was different; he did not hate de Montfort. This man detested his native country. There was a secret here somewhere. Corbett thought the matter would wait.

'Thank you, Master Ettrick.' As the man was about to leave, Corbett, using the same trick as with Plumpton, called him back.

'Master Ettrick, one matter. Did you know anything about the gift of wine to Sir Walter?'

'No, I did not.'

'Thank you. I may ask you to return.'

The priest turned his back and shrugged. 'Then you had better hurry up, Clerk, for the Earl of Surrey intends that I join his retinue and go back north to Scotland.'

'Do not worry,' Corbett jibed in return, 'I am sure this matter will soon be resolved.'

De Luce was next, different from the rest: cold, ascetic, a man fully in control of himself. He had a quick brain and was a born administrator, a shrewd assessor of character. Corbett reckoned de Luce to be about his own age, in his mid-thirties while the rest of the canons he had questioned, with the exception of Blaskett, were well past their fiftieth summer. Corbett asked the usual questions about the wine pannikin and the mass, but learned nothing new. De Luce could remember nothing unusual so Corbett turned to de Montfort's elusive private life.

'You are the cathedral treasurer?'

De Luce nodded.

'There were rumours about de Montfort's private life?'

'That is correct.'

'Was he associated with any squandering of money or funds?'

'No. The accounts were kept in good order. In fact,' de

Luce scratched his chin as if irritated by the question, 'de Montfort prided himself on not interfering with one penny of the cathedral's revenue. All money matters were left to me. He trusted me implicitly.'

'Was de Montfort a rich man?'

'Yes, very rich.'

'The source of his wealth?'

De Luce shrugged. 'He had a manor in Cathall, near the village of Leighton in Essex, but I never saw his accounts. He kept those himself.'

'A house?'

'Yes, he had a large house near Holborn but, as I have said, he kept his accounts to himself. They were distinct from those of the cathedral.'

'Did you know any of de Montfort's friends? A woman?'

De Luce's eyes narrowed. 'There were rumours, stories of scandal. I know what the others may have told you. I saw the same. A blowsy, rather overdressed woman who used to often meet him in the cathedral, but there is nothing scandalous in that. Is there, Clerk?'

'No, there isn't,' Corbett tartly replied. 'Fine, Sir Priest. I believe there is only Master Blaskett left.'

The young secretarius, when he entered, was nervous, his smooth, plump, olive-skinned face creased with concern, and he had his hands hidden in the sleeves of his robe. Corbett suspected this was to prevent him from seeing them tremble. He waved Blaskett to a seat.

'You were the dean's secretarius?'

The man nodded.

'Responsible for all letters sent out?'

'Yes, that is correct. I despatched and looked after all documents, memoranda, bills and indentures connected with the cathedral.'

'And how long have you held the post?'

'A year.'

'What was your relationship with your dean?'

The young man bowed his head and studied the table.

Corbett watched him.

'I asked you, sir, what was your relationship with your dean? Sir Philip Plumpton insinuated that the dean did not act as he should have done, either as a man or as a priest.'

Blaskett's eyes flickered up. Corbett noticed how long the lashes were, how girlish the eyes, now brimming with tears. Was this man strong enough to plan and carry out a blasphemous murder?

'The dean,' the secretarius began slowly, 'was a strange man, with strange desires, very secretive. I have held this benefice a year and never once did I see a document or write anything for him which could be held against him. Yet there was a ...' Blaskett paused. 'I do not mean to speak ill of the dead, but there was a smell of corruption about him. He was very friendly and sometimes when I was sitting writing he would stroke my hair. I objected. Plumpton, a man who loves listening to other people's conversations, heard the ensuing altercation.'

'And after that? I mean,' Corbett said, 'your relations with the dean?'

'Cold and formal. I think if he had lived,' Blaskett paused. 'I think if he had lived, perhaps I would have been dismissed from my post. Not from my prebend, but as a secretarius.'

'Do you know, Sir Stephen, anything which might solve this mystery of why de Montfort died? Who killed him? When and how?'

'No, I do not.'

Corbett looked at the scrap of parchment which bore the plan of where the celebrants stood at that fateful mass.

'Sir Stephen, may I remind you, that you were the last person to drink from the chalice before it was passed back to the dean.' Corbett stared at the young man. 'Some people might say because you held the chalice last, it gave you the opportunity to poison the wine.'

Blaskett almost sniggered. 'For a man who is a chief clerk in the king's chancery,' he said spitefully, 'you are peculiarly dull-witted. You have asked that question of all my colleagues and yet you consistently ignore one fact.'

'Which is?' Corbett snapped.

'After the mass was stopped and de Montfort's body was carried to the sacristy, I understand you examined the chalice and other sacred vessels on the altar?'

'That is correct.'

'I also saw the chalice later. Did you detect any sign of poison in the consecrated wine?'

'No, I did not.'

'Then how could I put poison in a cup from which de Montfort drank but which you later found to be free of poison? There is a conundrum there, Master Clerk. I think you should resolve that before you start implying, however much I may have disliked de Montfort, that I slipped poison into a sacred chalice during mass.'

Corbett stared at Blaskett. The young man's rather effeminate, childish approach was just a mask. In fact, he was probably the sharpest of all those he had interviewed and the riddle he posed could not be resolved. If the chalice was poisoned, why had he failed to detect poison in it when he examined the sacred vessels? Corbett mused on this puzzle for a few moments before continuing his interrogation.

'Sir Stephen,' Corbett said, 'it could well be that in the confusion and chaos following de Montfort's sudden death, somebody came back to the altar with another chalice.'

The young priest laughed.

'What are you saying? That there were two identical chalices? But that was de Montfort's. There are no two chalices in our inventory, or amongst the church plate, which are so similar. You are saying that someone, while people are rushing around the sanctuary examining de Monfort's body and taking it to the sacristy, someone came up with a similar cup, placed it on the altar and took the poisoned one away? And no one noticed? And that this person had such a chalice ready? I find that incredible.'

Corbett looked away and stared up at the rafters. It was

incredible but there was something, something Blaskett had touched on which stirred a memory. The thought eluded him. Something he had seen on that altar which was wrong, which should not have happened.

He glanced back at Blaskett. 'I thank you for pointing out the conundrum, Sir Stephen. I have finished with my questions. I would be most grateful if you could ask your colleagues to return.'

A few minutes later, the canons, all of them openly resentful at being summoned hither and thither by a man like Corbett, filed into the chamber and regrouped themselves around the table. Corbett asked a few desultory questions, particularly about de Montfort's wealth, before turning to Hervey.

'Master William, I would be grateful, once this is finished, if you would draw up a letter in the king's name and take it back to Westminster to seal, ordering the sheriffs and bailiffs of Essex to examine Cathall Manor and send to the Chancery immediately any reports they may have about Sir Walter de Montfort or his properties in Essex.'

The Clerk nodded.

Corbett turned back to the ring of hostile faces.

'Sir Philip, you have a servant?' Plumpton nodded.

'Did de Montfort?'

'It is strange you ask that,' John de Eveden, the librarian broke in. 'He was such a secretive man. He had servitors in the cathedral to attend to his every wish but not one body servant, not like the rest of us.'

Corbett nodded, that would fit de Montfort's character. A man who had a very private life, surrounded by rumour and scandal, would never entrust his reputation to the gossip of a body servant.

'Why do you ask?' Ettrick demanded, his voice rising. 'Why do you ask such a question? Talk to us. We are intelligent men, Master Corbett. We can give intelligent answers to intelligent questions.'

'I am not demeaning your intelligence,' Corbett said firmly. 'But I would like to interview all those servants who had the right to come in and out of the chapter-house, as well as into the cathedral, without notice being raised.'

This was quickly agreed. The canons gave Blaskett the task of calling and organizing the servants. Corbett dismissed Hervey, sending him back to Westminster, though he kept the clerk's notes. After that, Corbett and Ranulf spent the rest of the morning sitting in the chapter-house, interviewing at least a dozen servitors, male and female. The women – laundresses and cleaners he dismissed immediately – for they would have no right to go into the sacristy or any of the canons' chambers. The men were mainly those who had fought in the king's wars, veterans who had been given a post in the cathedral as a reward for services. Old, rheumy-eyed and garrulous, some displayed the most horrific scars and wounds. Corbett dealt with them quickly, asking two questions: first, did they carry any wine down to the vestry room on the morning de Montfort died? The answer was always no. The second, did they go into the sacristy or vestry after de Montfort's death? Again, the answer was no. They had seen nothing untoward. Corbett pronounced himself satisfied. The bells began to ring for the midday service of nones and the canons began to file back into the choir to sing divine office. Corbett and Ranulf decided to leave. Plumpton hurried up to them, effusive in his warmth.

'Master Corbett, Master Corbett.'

'Yes, Sir Philip?'

'Perhaps you would like to see de Montfort's chamber?'

Corbett shrugged. 'Of course.'

He was led up a stone spiral staircase to the floor above the chapter-house, a long, white-washed passage broken up by shiny, lozenge-shaped wooden doors.

'Each of these,' Philip said with some pride, 'belongs to one of the canons. De Montfort's is here.' He turned to his immediate left and, after searching for a key on the massive iron ring which swung from his belt, he opened the door and they entered.

The room was opulent, luxurious. Two oval-shaped windows were made of pure glass, one of them stained, depicting a scene from the Bible. Corbett thought it was Jonah being delivered from the whale. The huge, four poster bed was covered with an ermine, gold-fringed coverlet. The heavy blue curtains which usually cordoned it off were pulled back to display red and white bolsters. A silver crucifix hung on the wall. Beside the bed was a small table with a two-branched silver candelabra; a huge chest lay against the far wall under the windows with another at the foot of the bed. A peg was fitted into the wall for cloaks and other garments.

Corbett turned. 'May I?' Without waiting for an answer, he lifted up the lid of the trunk at the end of the bed, noting how the lock had been broken. Inside there was nothing much: bits and pieces, belts, buckles, a pair of Spanish soft riding boots. Corbett noted two books; one a Bible, the other containing the divine office.

'We broke the lock,' Plumpton said, 'to ensure there was nothing precious, nothing of interest.'

Corbett nodded and walked across to the larger trunk. This, too, had had its lock broken. He raised the lid and, despite the murmur of protest from Plumpton, went through the layers of clothing in it, but there was nothing. He closed it and stared once more round the room.

'Master de Montfort liked his comforts?'

'Yes, he did,' Plumpton replied. 'But I assure you, Master Clerk, we have been through this room. There is nothing here that would interest you.'

'Why did you go through it?' Corbett snapped.

Plumpton shrugged. 'De Montfort died; we had to make an inventory of his belongings.'

'Was the chalice kept here? I mean, the one he used at mass?'

'Oh, no,' Plumpton said, 'I am the sacristan. Canon Law

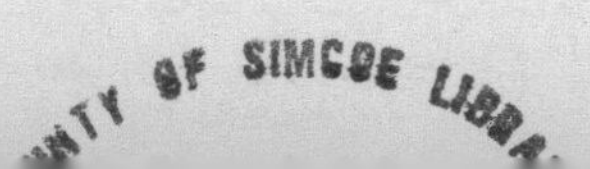

insists such sacred vessels are always kept in or near the church under lock and key. De Montfort himself enforced that rule.'

Corbett smiled and strode out. They went down the stairs, the clerk thanking the priest for his attention and help and, followed by a rather bemused Ranulf, Corbett left the cathedral precincts.

10

Corbett and Ranulf entered Paternoster Row and walked on into Cheapside. The streets were already filling up with people. The sky was bright blue and a warmish sun was gradually melting the snow so that it fell off the sloping roofs, crashing into the streets below. Londoners had decided to take advantage of the fair weather and Cheapside was thronged. Shop fronts were down and booths erected, the striped awnings flapping in a strong breeze. The goldsmiths, pelterers, furriers and parchment-sellers were all busy, intent on recovering the business lost during the bad weather. Ladies in fur-lined cloaks tripped through the snow followed by anxious maids; lawyers, making their way up into the nave of St Paul's to do business, swaggered haughtily by. There were men-at-arms from the Palace and Tower. Young children were everywhere and apprentices ran out from behind the booths, trying to catch the attention of would-be purchasers. Two beggars staggered by, each holding the other, for the ground underfoot was slippery. Now and again, snow would fall onto a striped awning to the anguished yell of a shopkeeper and the ecstatic cries of the urchins who swarmed everywhere.

Corbett felt as if he had come into a different world. St Paul's had been cold, dark, still in the icy grip of winter. Here, everything was bright, full of life, movement and colour. He and Ranulf forced their way through the crowds. Most people tried to keep to the centre of the street, well away from the sloping roofs and the ever falling snow. Shoemakers hammered away at their benches. Carters, having brought their goods into the city through the snow, had decided to celebrate and the taverns had no need to hang out garlands or signs to attract custom. The Sun on the Hoop, The Cock, The Red Door, The Bell and The Cat and Fiddle, were all doing a roaring trade. The cooks and valets stood outside the doors shouting, 'Hot pies!'; 'Hot good pies and cheese!'; 'Come and dine!'; and competed with cries of 'White wine of Alsace!'; 'Red wine of Gascony!': 'Wine of the Rhine!'; 'Wine of Rochelle!' The cold, the smells of cooking and the loud cries reminded Corbett how hungry he was. He stopped beside a fish stall to watch a furious debate between two vendors, which broke into a fight. One man was sent crashing against the wooden framework, spilling onto the slushy ground his wares of cod, salmon, conger, ray, sturgeon, herring, pilchards, and sprats. Immediately, these were picked up by urchins and, to the anguished cry of their owner, taken off without a 'by your leave' or a penny paid.

Corbett, usually a solitary man, often enjoyed mingling with the crowds and watching the different scenes. On one corner he saw a corpse lying covered in a rough awning. Around it the Wardman had called twelve people to sit in judgement. Some unfortunate had evidently dropped dead or been killed in a brawl and the local coroner was now empanelling a jury of twelve men to decide on the cause of death and what procedures should be followed.

Down the middle of Cheapside came a cart covered with a black cloth on which a white cross was painted. The horse, moving slowly and dolefully, had a bell on its bridle which tolled mournfully. A Carthusian monk carefully led the beast through the slush and dirt of the street. A bare-headed and bare-footed sanctuary man who had agreed to abjure the kingdom, his legs and ankles purple with the cold, walked down the street carrying a wooden cross before him, on his way to Bridgegate and accompanied by the serjeant of his ward. Apparently, he was a murderer who had taken sanctuary but then released himself from it by promising to abjure the kingdom. Corbett knew the felon had three days to reach Dover and quietly concluded that there was very little chance he would reach it: either he would die in the intense cold or the relatives of the person he had murdered would follow and kill him in some lonely spot.

For a few moments, the hubbub of the market-place died as a city officer, clad in a tunic decorated with a death's-head and grinning skulls, came up and rang a bell, proclaiming in a booming voice, 'Good people, of your charity, pray, for the soul of our dear brother, Robert Hinckley, who departed this life at nine o' clock last evening.'

The people round Corbett murmured a prayer and the death crier passed on. Corbett decided to dally amongst the stalls. Perhaps he could pick up something, a gift for Maeve, from the woollen caps, laces, ribbons, fringes of silk, thread, twine, silk, laces of gold, rings of copper, candlesticks, ewers, brushes, iron, – anything that she might find useful. He bought a small brooch, in the form of a cross with a dragon twisted round it, made out of hammered gold and attached to a fine silk-like chain. Corbett placed this carefully in his pouch, keeping his hand over it, for the place swarmed with cutpurses and pick-pockets also intent on making up any losses they had suffered during the heavy snowfall.

Feeling hungry, he and Ranulf headed for a tavern. Inside, it was dank but warm and rather musty with a fire blazing in the huge grate in the far wall. Corbett, ignoring the evil-smelling rushes, chose a table far away from the other revellers, a group of dicers and a young woman who already looked far gone in her cups. The landlord, a stocky fellow with an apron tied round his waist, came up, his greasy hands held out in welcome. He offered sweet wines from Cyprus and Sicily but Corbett simply ordered two plates of meat and ale, warmed and heavily spiced.

While they were eating Corbett nudged Ranulf. 'This morning, in the cathedral, did you learn anything I may have missed?'

His servant shook his head and stuck his nose back in the tankard.

'You are sure?' Corbett persisted.

Ranulf deliberated, enjoying this rare moment. Corbett asking for his advice.

'There was one thing,' he said slowly.

'What was that?'

'At the altar,' Ranulf used the plates and tankards on the table as symbols, 'De Montfort stood in the centre?'

'Yes,' Corbett replied impatiently.

'The two, one on each side. They would have stood close?'

Corbett nodded.

'Then it is possible,' Ranulf said, 'for one of them, or both, to place the poison in the chalice when it was returned?'

Corbett grimaced. 'True. But still there is the great mystery, what Blaskett called the conundrum. What happened to the poisoned wine? When I examined the chalice, the wine was untainted and there was no smell to it at all.' Corbett still felt there was something just outside his grasp, something he had seen on that altar and it nagged at him now.

He put down the tankard and leaned back on his stool against the wall. There was something wrong. He remembered the wine drops on the floor and the other drops which smelt of the poison on the altar frontal. Someone must have changed cups. But how had it been done? Surely, there were not two chalices? He had established that. He rose, tossed a few coins at the tavern-keeper and left, bidding Ranulf to take care of himself while he slowly walked back to his lodgings. There, having lit a candle and brought out his writing tray and scraps of parchment, Corbett began to list what he knew so far.

Item De Montfort had been poisoned during mass.

Item De Montfort was a man with a secret and private life. There were few details known about him except his liaison with the strange woman who had been seen on the edge of the sanctuary the day the priest had died.

Item De Montfort was disliked by most of his colleagues and seemed to have no friends.

Item De Montfort was supposed to give a sermon after the mass denouncing royal taxation. Instead, Edward had bribed him to give a speech confirming the king's right to tax the church.

Item If de Montfort was poisoned, how?

Item Why was it only de Montfort (who only drank from the chalice) killed yet not any of the priests celebrating mass with him?

Item If de Montfort was poisoned from the chalice, what had happened to the poisoned wine?

Item There could have been two cups. But who exchanged them and when? Was it possible that an exact replica had been made?

The next morning Corbett rose early. He did not bother to call on Ranulf but, dressing in his best robes, made his way out into the streets. Plumpton had told him that de Montfort's funeral mass was to be held at eleven that morning. Corbett made his way slowly back to the cathedral, the problems he had listed the night before still ringing in his head. This was a mystery, one he could not fathom, but he felt that if he had the missing pieces then the puzzle would fall into place. He walked up a still-deserted Cheapside. There were only a few beggars scurrying about; a baker stood in the stocks, next to him a fishmonger. The latter had sold stale fish, a serious offence in the city, as many doctors believed it was a cause of leprosy. The fishmonger stood there, hands and head caught in the iron clasp of the stocks, whilst beneath his nose hung a rotten fish. The baker next to him looked equally doleful. A sign had also been looped round his head. It said that Thomas-atte-Criche, baker, had been found guilty of the serious crime of stealing dough. Corbett looked at the man's miserable face.

'What did you do?' he asked, using the edge of his robe to wipe away some of the man's sweat.

'My servant,' the man gasped. 'People brought dough into our bakery. They put it on the table. I was supposed to put it into pans for baking but I had a secret door in the table. My apprentice would sit underneath the table and remove parts of the dough. I would then bake the loaves and give them to the women who had brought me their dough. The rest I would collect, bake fresh bread and sell it.' The baker spat. 'I should not have trusted that apprentice. He turned on me.' He looked lugubriously at Corbett, his fleshy face ashen with the pain of the iron clasp round his neck. 'I must stand here till sunset.'

Corbett nodded sympathetically and passed on; the man would not have to stand long; on a winter's day sunset would be early.

Corbett reached Paternoster Row and went into the cathedral grounds, the gates having been opened as soon as prime was finished. At the doors, vergers were in attendance. Corbett whispered to one and was allowed up into the nave. Sconce lights had been lit in the choir sanctuary and the great candles on the high altar flared and dipped against the darkness. The stalls were already filling with the cantors for the mass, and between the choir and the steps of the sanctuary stood de Montfort's coffin. Corbett walked up and studied it; made of polished pinewood, it rested on crimson-draped trestles. On each side of the coffin, purple candles flickered in black wrought-iron candlesticks. Someone had placed a flower on the coffin-lid. Corbett looked around and glimpsed in the far corner, near where she had stood before, the woman he had last seen on the day de Montfort died. There were a few other people, mostly mere spectators, stark proof that the dead man had had few friends. Corbett was about to go across to the woman but she suddenly turned on her heel and walked quickly down the nave. Corbett watched her go and, leaning against a pillar, waited for mass to commence.

At last the Requiem began. Like the mass Corbett had attended with the king many days earlier, it was celebrated by five or six canons, the main celebrant being Sir Philip Plumpton. Corbett had to refrain from smiling, Plumpton had hated the dead man, yet here he was interceding before God for de Montfort's soul. The requiems were sung, the coffin blessed, incensed and taken out into the graveyard on the shoulders of six stout men, preceded by vergers and servants of the cathedral, bearing banners depicting the Virgin Mary, St George and St Paul. These three standard-bearers walked ahead of Plumpton, followed by other canons and a group of young boys, all dressed in white, bearing tapers. The coffin was surrounded by torch bearers, fifty-six in number, each representing a year of the deceased man's life. The bier, now covered with costly cloths of gold, was followed by a group of ladies sobbing loudly, all dressed completely in black with lace veils over their heads. Corbett dismissed them with a supercilious glance as professional mourners. He had no time for people who profited from the dead. He watched as the long sorrowful procession wound its way out of the cathedral to a far corner in the grounds, where a fresh mound of earth denoted de Montfort's last resting-place.

Corbett stood by the door hearing faintly the mumblings of Plumpton as once again he asked God to take his beloved servant, Walter de Montfort, into his safe-keeping. The body was lowered into the ground, Corbett heard the clumps of earth falling on the wooden coffin-lid and the procession came back into the cathedral. Corbett sensed the mourners' relief that it was all over. The door closed and from outside Corbett heard the faint clatter of the spades as the grave-diggers covered the coffin. He waited for a respectful while before walking across the sanctuary; there, he genuflected before the winking light and went into the sacristy. Plumpton was divesting, amice, alb, stole, all the paraphernalia priests seemed to think they needed when they spoke to God. The priest knew Corbett was behind him but the clerk had to wait until Plumpton was divested and only then did he greet him.

'Master Corbett, I cannot say it's a pleasure to see you again.'

'Sir Philip,' Corbett replied cheerily. 'I am here on the king's business.' On any other occasion Plumpton would have groaned out loud for he had begun to hate this inquisitive, hard-faced, cat-eyed clerk who would not leave the dead alone and kept coming back to ask questions.

'What is it?' Plumpton snapped.

'On behalf of the king, I would like you and the other four celebrants of the mass officiating when de Montfort died, to join me in the sanctuary.'

'What is this?' Plumpton stepped back, his eyes narrowed in amazement. 'Why don't you leave this terrible business alone?'

'Why not ask the king?' Corbett said. 'You will have the opportunity if you refuse.' Plumpton sighed, and spun on his heel and stomped out.

Corbett stood looking round the sacristy, at the cupboards, the huge leather iron-bound chests, all padlocked, some of them with three, even four clasps; the barrels full of candles of various hues denoting their purity; boxes of sanctuary lights, tapers, casks of incense, nothing of real interest. He walked to where Plumpton had left a huge cupboard unlocked and pulled the door open. Inside were all the vestments the priests used in their services, each arranged in colours denoting the different liturgical seasons of the year. On the far left he saw the chasubles which had been used at that fatal mass and, going deeper into the cupboard, examined each of them minutely. One of them caught his attention and he studied the stain on it. Then, breathing quickly with excitement, Corbett closed the door as he heard footsteps in the passageway outside. Plumpton, accompanied by the other canons, stormed into the room. They were all angry at being called away from their different duties to dance attendance yet again on a common clerk. He could read their minds and knew the rancour they must feel for him. Only Blaskett and de Luce seemed calm.

Corbett waited for a while before speaking.

'Sir Philip, if you would, please.' He stepped aside and Plumpton brushed past him, the others following up the sanctuary steps, until they all stood before the altar. Corbett, who had picked up a plain pewter cup he had seen lying in the sacristy, asked the canons to arrange themselves as they were at the fateful mass, whilst he took the place of de Montfort. Once they had done so, Corbett made them go through the rite of communion. The cup was passed down, first to those on his right, de Eveden and Ettrick, the latter sent it back across the altar to Blaskett, who passed it to de Luce, Plumpton and so back to Corbett. One thing the clerk did notice, Ranulf was right: shielded by the rest, either de Eveden or Plumpton could have administered poison without the others noticing, though there was still the risk of alerting de Montfort. Moreover, if Plumpton or de Eveden was the poisoner, each would have noticed the other. Did the two conspire together? Corbett dismissed the thought as too fanciful, for the two men disliked each other intensely. There was no comradeship there, no feeling of conspiracy. Corbett was about to thank and dismiss them when suddenly a voice called out behind him.

'And the Angel of the Lord came down into the sanctuary and cleansed it with his sword!' Corbett turned and looked towards the anchor house. There in the slit he could see the bright eyes of the hermit glaring out at him. Corbett went down the stairs.

'What is it you want, man of God? Who is God's angel?'

'Why,' the anchorite's voice rang out clear as a bell, 'it is you, God's emissary sent to bring justice, and if not God's at least the king's.'

'Then, if you can see things so clearly,' Corbett said wryly, on the point of spinning on his heel and walking back to join the rest, 'could you not see who actually killed de Montfort?'

'I can see what you have been doing,' the voice replied. 'I have been working on the conundrum facing you.'

'And what is the solution?'

'Quite simple. You are wondering how the others could drink from the chalice after de Montfort, yet they live but he died. Am I not correct?'

Corbett nodded, watching the eyes intently.

'But they have not told you. Ask them.'

'Ask them what?'

'Ask them how many times de Montfort drank from the cup. Remind them of their Canon Law. Before a chalice is given as a symbol of peace, the celebrant always drinks a second time. The first time he drinks at the communion, the second time as the symbol of the kiss of peace. Why not ask them?'

Corbett twisted round and looked up at the canons. They had no need to answer, it was written in all of their faces.

'Sir priests,' he called out. 'It would be best if you waited for me. Perhaps in the sacristy.'

This time they went as dutifully and meekly as lambs.

Corbett moved closer to the anchorite's gap.

'Tell me, man of God, what did you see? Is there anything else I should know? What happened when de Montfort collapsed?'

All he received in reply was a quiet chuckle.

'Tell me,' Corbett insisted.

'I saw nothing,' the anchorite replied slowly. 'When de Montfort fell, so did I, on my knees here in my cell, to pray God would have mercy on his sinful soul. That is all the help I can give. Except one thing. Take care, Master Clerk. These canons wish you dead.'

11

Corbett, feeling angry and secretly alarmed, mumbled his thanks to the anchorite and strode back into the sacristy. The canons stood there like boys caught in some mischief. None of them would meet his eye.

'So,' Corbett began, 'we have a little mystery here.' He felt beneath his cloak, drew out his sword and held it up by the cross-hilt. 'I swear,' he said, 'unless you tell me the truth, now, about what you saw, felt or heard on that altar when de Montfort died, I swear by Christ's cross, I will see you all in the Tower by sunset!' He glared at each of them, sheathed his sword and leant against the corner of the table, arms folded. Plumpton came forward, licking his lips nervously.

'The anchorite spoke the truth,' he began. 'He must have seen it. One thing an anchorite always demands is a clear view of the altar, in order to see the cross as well as reverence the elevated host and chalice. De Montfort did drink twice from the chalice. You will find that in Canon Law he must.' He looked towards Ettrick. 'De Montfort in fact forgot. It was Sir David here who came across and reminded him.'

'Is that right, Ettrick?' Corbett snapped. The Scotsman nodded.

'I saw the chalice come back. De Montfort was about to turn to take it down the sanctuary steps. I went across and whispered in his ear. To an onlooker it would appear I was helping him in the rite. He raised the chalice, drank from it, the rest you know.'

'Do I?' Corbett said sharply. 'Is there anything else I should know?' No one answered. 'Is there anything else I should know?' he repeated. There was silence.

Corbett looked at Plumpton.

'Well, Sir Philip, there are a few more questions I would like to ask but, before I do that, I would like to remind you, Sir John,' he turned to the librarian, 'that you were the last person to hold the chalice before de Montfort drank from it.'

Sir John's face was a mask of tragedy. 'But that is not fair,' he spluttered. 'That is not fair. Your words are barbs.'

'Once I have solved the mystery,' Corbett replied, 'then these questions will stop. But, Sir Philip, you said de Montfort, like you all, kept the precious plate with which he used to celebrate mass here in the sacristy.'

Plumpton nodded.

'I would like to see it.'

Sir Philip took a bunch of keys from his belt and went to a chest in the far corner. It was made of leather and wood, bound by strips of iron and secured by four locks. Each needed a separate key. Once all the locks had been unclasped, Plumpton pulled back the lid and Corbett had to stifle his cry of astonishment at the gorgeous plate stored there, a treasure hoard even the king would have envied. Jewelled monstrances, golden patens, silver dishes, at least a dozen precious cups. Some were in pouches of red Spanish leather, others in boxes, but most just lay where they had been carelessly tossed. The inside of the trunk was lined with thick samite.

Sir Philip moved the cups around carefully before pulling one out. Corbett recognized the chalice he had held the morning de Montfort had died. Plumpton brought it across to Corbett. A beautiful piece of craftmanship, Corbett thought it must be at least a hundred years old. The cup was of pure gold, the stem and base of thick silver encrusted with gold and precious gems. He turned it over and saw the goldmaker's hallmark displayed on the base. The inside of the cup was beaten gold, pure, bright, so it caught the light of the candles. Corbett held it up to his nose and sniffed; there was a faint smell of polish and sweetened wine but nothing else. He moved it from one hand to the other, feeling its worth.

'There is no other cup like this?' he asked, returning it to Plumpton. A chorus of denials greeted him.

'The cup,' de Eveden said hastily, trying to be of help, 'is unique. Only a master craftsman could have made it. It would be recognized anywhere as de Montfort's cup.'

Corbett nodded.

'There is one other matter. When de Montfort died, he must have left some papers?'

'Yes,' Plumpton said. 'We have them stored down in the treasure room. We have to draw up an inventory for the city sheriff and other officials.'

'Why was I not shown these?' Corbett asked. 'You showed me his chamber readily enough.' He looked around the sacristy. 'This place will do as good as any. I want those papers brought here. Now!'

Plumpton was about to protest but, after one look at Corbett, he changed his mind. He indicated a chair and table and hurried off. Corbett dismissed the rest, gratified to see they left the sacristy a little less arrogantly than when they had entered. At last Plumpton, followed by three servants huffing and blowing under the weight of a large leather-bound chest, returned. Corbett pointed to the table, on which the servants placed the chest and left the room. Corbett opened the lid.

'These are all de Montfort's documents?'

'All his moveables,' Plumpton replied, using the legal term. 'This is everything that de Montfort had, apart from his clothing, which you have seen. A number of books are here, all his papers and precious objects.'

'Fine. If you would, Sir Philip, continue your kindness by lighting more candles and having a brazier placed here, perhaps a little wine? I will go through the contents of this trunk and then you may have it back.' And, not waiting for an answer from the priest, Corbett began to unpack the large chest.

After three hours' searching Corbett concluded it contained little of importance. Apart from a large account-book there was nothing: pieces of parchment filled with notes, sets of prayer beads, a broken crucifix. The remaining documents were bills and memoranda but nothing to excite any interest. Corbett sent for Plumpton, whom he informed that he had finished, though he would take the ledger-book home for personal study. Sir Philip protested loudly but Corbett reminded him that his commission was from the king and, if he had any protests or objections, it was useless making them to the king's messenger but to go direct to His Grace at Westminster. Plumpton, looking very subdued, shouted for the servants to refill the trunk and swept out of the room. Corbett was also about to leave when he heard a faint knock on the door.

'Come in.' The door opened and John de Eveden, the librarian, entered like some contrite boy coming to apologize. He sat down on a stool just inside the door, his hands folded in his lap. Corbett stood, wrapping his cloak around him, toying with the clasp.

'Sir John, you wish to speak to me.'

The canon nodded.

'What is the matter, man?' Corbett asked. 'You come in here like a maid who has a confession to make.'

'I am no maid,' de Eveden said wryly. 'But I do have a confession.'

'Then give it.'

'I did not drink the wine.'

'What do you mean?'

'When the chalice was passed back, I did not drink the wine.'

Corbett went over and looked down at de Eveden. 'Why not?'

The priest shrugged. 'You laypeople do not know what it is like to be a priest,' he replied. 'You pass judgement on us. Hold us up as perfect specimens yet attack us when we are not. I am no different. My weakness, Master Clerk, or my weakness was, the grape, the wine. I used to spend days, long nights, drinking cup after cup – it was my only vice. I took an oath one night after I had drunk too much and found myself in circumstances I cannot describe. I crawled like a child into the sanctuary and took an oath. I would not drink wine ever again be it consecrated or not. That's all you should know.' He shrugged. 'I did not drink the wine de Montfort drank.'

Corbett stared down at him. Deep in his heart he felt the man might be telling the truth but he did wonder why, and why now.

'Tell me, Sir John,' he said, 'when de Montfort died and collapsed, what happened?'

'We stood around. I did not know what had happened, nor did my brethren.' De Eveden passed a hand over his eyes. 'All was confusion, chaos, I cannot remember. People rushing here and there.'

'Did you see anyone go to the altar?'

'No, I did not.'

'Nothing strange?'

'No, I did not,' de Eveden said firmly.

'The gossips amongst your brethren. Did they see anything strange?'

De Eveden looked sharply at Corbett. 'No, they did not. I swear that I have heard nothing, nothing extraordinary, nothing strange.'

'Tell me,' Corbett said, 'how were you dressed for mass? What did each of the celebrants wear?'

De Eveden spread his hands. 'The usual garments. We wore our robes and over them the long, white alb fastened by a gold cord, the amice, a strip of silk on our wrists, the stole about our necks. Over that the chasuble. Why?'

'Nothing,' Corbett replied. 'The chasubles? They are kept

here?'

'Yes, they are.'

'And the albs, the white tunics worn under them?'

The librarian shrugged. 'As usual, they are passed to the laundress. She washes and presses them and that is the end of the matter. Why?'

'Nothing,' Corbett replied. 'You have told me all.'

Corbett left the librarian and strode out across the sanctuary and empty choir into the nave of the church. The business for the day was finishing; lawyers and parchment sellers were drifting off, and the twelve scribes, who sold their services to anyone who wished a letter written, were packing away their writing trays in small leather cases.

As Corbett was going out of the main west door, a hand caught his shoulder. He whirled, his hand going beneath his cloak for his dagger but, in the fading light, he recognized the fleshy, still beautiful face of the courtesan.

'What do you want, woman?' he demanded.

'You should not be so aggressive, Clerk,' she replied. 'I know you are probably asking questions about me so I thought I should come and introduce myself.'

'And your name?'

'Abigail. What do you want with me?'

'What did the Dean of St Paul's, Walter de Montfort, want with you?'

The woman smiled. 'What any man does.'

'And what is that?'

'You are still too aggressive, Master Clerk. What is your name?'

'Hugh Corbett, senior clerk in the Chancery.' The woman mimicked his words. It was so accurate that, in spite of himself, Corbett smiled.

'I am sorry,' he said. 'I am cold. I don't like the task in which I am involved and I am tired. If you wish to play games then perhaps another time, but not now.'

'Tush, man.' The woman put an ermine-gloved hand on

Corbett's wrist. 'I only thought it was a matter of time before you came to see me so I thought I would do the courtesy of saving you a visit.'

'Fine,' Corbett said. 'But the question still stands. What was your relationship with Walter de Montfort?'

'Simple,' the woman said. 'I hold his house in Candlewick Street.'

'What do you mean, you hold it?'

'He rents it to me.'

'What is so special about that?'

'Oh, you have never been to my house, Master Clerk, but if you did, you would notice that there are many bedrooms, all of them luxuriously furnished.'

'You mean it's a brothel,' Corbett said, immediately regretting his brusqueness as the woman's eyes flinched with pain. Corbett looked steadily at her. Undoubtedly she had once been a most beautiful woman; her face was still heart-shaped, her eyes grey and well spaced; she had a perfectly formed nose and a mouth surely created for kissing. She was quick and intelligent, in a way reminding him of Maeve, with her tart replies and her ability to hold her own in any debate.

'And de Montfort,' Corbett said slowly, 'he knew you ran his house as a brothel?'

'Of course. He took half the profits.'

Corbett threw his head back and laughed. People leaving the cathedral stared at him, laughing so loudly in his dark-coloured clothes; it rang like a bell through the twilight. The woman smiled too.

'What is so amusing?' she asked.

Corbett wiped his mouth with his hand. 'In this world,' he said, 'nothing is ever what it seems to be. Look,' he said, 'tell me about de Montfort.'

She shrugged. 'As any man, he sunned himself like a barnyard cock strutting on his dunghill. He played his roles, acted out his parts. You see it all the time, Master Corbett. De Montfort in his robes up on the high altar – I have seen him in less, how can we say, celebrated positions. And yet,' she continued, 'he is no different from others. No different from the king, who pursues justice yet squeezes taxes from his people; or a knight who wears the red cross of the Crusaders and grabs a sword to hack down people for sweet Jesus's sake; or a priest who pretends that he is better than anyone else, yet who is far worse for not practising what he preaches.' She edged a little closer so Corbett could see the pale creaminess of her skin and catch the fragrance of her perfume. 'What are you, Master Clerk?' She gazed steadily into his eyes. 'No, you are not a barnyard cock,' she said. 'You are a hawk. You sit high up in the tree and survey everything with cold detachment; functional, you carry out your tasks.'

Corbett would have retorted angrily to anyone else, but the woman's wit and strength of character had left him virtually speechless.

'Well, Master Corbett. Now you know who I am and my relationship with de Montfort.'

'One question,' Corbett said. 'Are you glad he is dead?'

He saw the hate blaze like a fire in the woman's eyes.

'Yes, I am,' she replied fiercely. 'He was a cruel villain. He cheated me, persecuted me and, unless I followed instructions to the letter, threatened me with beadles, officials and a public whipping through the streets. He was always there with his hand out, ensuring I gave him half of what I earned. Yes, I am glad he is dead. Whoever killed him performed me a favour. If they hadn't done it, Master Clerk, believe me, in time I would have.' And, spinning on her heel, her skirts billowing around her, she clattered down the steps. Corbett called after her.

'Abigail.'

The woman stopped and turned, a faint smile on her lips. 'Yes, Master Clerk?'

'There are probably only five honest people in this city and you must be one of them.'

Her smile widened, revealing perfect white teeth.

'Perhaps we may meet again, Clerk, in more comfortable surroundings.'

Corbett grinned, but the woman, not waiting for a reply, disappeared into the darkness.

* * *

Compline had been sung at St Paul's and the canons had filed out, some to the refectory, others to their own chambers; the doors were closed and locked. Outside the snow-packed earth gleamed under the light of a full moon and a wind had sprung up, its eerie noise singing around the building, making it creak and groan. Even the hardened sanctuary men, who lived amongst the graves in the derelict huts near the huge curtain wall, shivered and pulled their rags closer about them and vowed they would not go out on such a night. During the day St Paul's was a bustle of activity, but this only masked the feeling of menace, of ominous silence, which fell once the cathedral was closed.

The sanctuary men would have been even more frightened if they had got within the locked church and seen the cowled figure crouching at the base of a pillar and singing a hymn softly to himself as he glared into the darkness. The man stopped his humming and chewed his lip thoughtfully. He really should not be here, but it was the best place to think. Plots and plans, like bats, seemed to move more smoothly at night. He had not intended to kill de Montfort though he was glad the silly, prattling hypocrite was dead. The figure cursed his own mistakes: Edward of England should have collapsed in the presence of his subjects, lay and spiritual. All would have seen it as God's judgement, and his brother's death and those of his wife and little ones would have been avenged.

The man raised his head and peered deeply into the darkness. He had heard stories that the cathedral was built over the original place of a temple dedicated to Diana and he wondered if the old demons lingered still. If he could, he would call up these demons and offer them his soul in exchange for Edward's downfall. There would be other opportunities for that, however. He must first deal with that meddling clerk, Corbett. The man bit fiercely at the skin on his thumb but felt no pain. God, how he hated that interfering clerk! There was something cold and detached about him, with his long dark face, black tousled hair and those eyes, like a cat's, slanted, green, ever watchful. The man rubbed his hands and smiled. Yes, he would have to do something about Corbett and it would have to be done very soon.

12

Corbett spent the next three days going through de Montfort's accounts. They were really quite crude, written on pieces of parchment stitched together with heavy twine. They did not refer to the abbey but simply listed expenses, though a great deal of the money had been deposited with different bankers. Corbett idly wondered how many of these would admit to holding monies on behalf of the priest. The income fascinated him, coming as it did from several sources. One was minor: stipends, benefices, gifts from people and close relatives, nothing much, but a sharp contrast to the rest. Every quarter there were huge amounts, literally hundreds of pounds sterling in bags of silver from two places: Cathall Manor in Essex and from his property in London.

Corbett knew the secret of de Montfort's London houses but he wondered what was so special about Cathall. Corbett considered travelling there to find out but, after many journeys downstairs to inspect the weather, realized it could change again and he did not wish to be cut off in some village in Essex. Moreover, if the thaw continued, his letters would soon reach the sheriff and other officials in Essex and they would collect the necessary information on his behalf. He wondered about Ranulf's recent, fitful appearances; on one occasion to change his clothes, another to beg Corbett for some money which the clerk absentmindedly gave. He never enquired too much into Ranulf's whereabouts; he had told him bluntly not to break the law and, apart from that, left him to his own conscience and confessor. Corbett had a shrewd idea, however, that Ranulf was a man totally dedicated to the pleasures of the flesh, having seen him flirt dangerously with other men's wives and daughters.

In this the clerk was correct, for Ranulf was busy pursuing the plump-haunched, arrogant young wife of a London mercer. He had wooed and pursued her for days and felt sure his quarry would be brought down. On that particular Sunday evening, however, Ranulf returned, minus one boot, to his lodgings in Bread Street. Corbett was too immersed in his own thoughts to pay much attention and Ranulf was not humble enough to admit that he had been in the lady's chamber preparing for a night of pleasure when her husband, reportedly away on business, had returned unexpectedly because of bad weather. Ranulf had had to flee, the anguished screams and the angry roars of the couple behind still ringing in his ears.

Ranulf slunk back to his lodgings, anxious lest his master interrogate him, but Corbett was still trying to reconstruct what had happened at the high altar of St Paul's.

First, he listed what each priest had worn: a white alb bound by a cord over which there was a chasuble; the thick gold jewel-encrusted cope displaying the colour of the day's feast; a matching stole round the neck and an amice. Corbett remembered the copes and chasubles he had seen in the cupboard in the sacristy of St Paul's, thick, heavy, encrusted with jewels.

Secondly, he looked at the plan of the celebrants that day. On the far right of de Montfort had been de Eveden and the Scotsman, Ettrick. On the far left the young man, Blaskett, de Luce and Plumpton. Once again Corbett traced the way the chalice would have been passed. First, up to Ettrick, and then back along to Plumpton, de Luce and Blaskett before it was returned by de Luce and Plumpton to de Montfort who had taken the fatal sip. According to de Eveden he had not drunk from the chalice. Corbett wondered whether to believe him. He was sure, during the feast after the mass at which de Montfort had died, he had seen de Eveden drinking. So was the librarian lying? If he was not, the logical explanation would be that the chalice had been poisoned by Blaskett or de Luce. But there again, Plumpton on de Montfort's left, could be the secret assassin. Moreover, de Eveden may not have drunk from the chalice, but that did not stop him from poisoning it.

Corbett looked again at the diagram. He tried to reconstruct the altar as he had seen it when the king had sent him back to assess everything. He had seen something odd which was now mysteriously plaguing him, something very wrong. He remembered the stains on the altar frontal and the wine on the carpet. His mind chased the problem. He felt like a dog, loose in a forest chasing shadows, nothing substantial, except there was something evil about St Paul's. Perhaps, as a good servant of the king, he should insist that the whole college of canons be investigated by the Bishop of London and have the evil rooted out, for there was something malevolent beyond the normal animosities, jealousies and rivalries one would find in any small, enclosed community.

Corbett spent most of Sunday evening attempting to solve the puzzle, but he failed to reach a satisfactory conclusion. At last, he put down his pen, opened the shutters of his room and looked out over the city. A heavy mist had rolled in across the Thames, blanketing out the sky so that he could only see the odd winking glare of a fire or the lights of lanterns placed outside doors by householders. He wanted this matter finished. He thought of Ranulf upstairs and envied the young man's exuberance for every waking moment. Corbett looked up, the same sky now shrouded Maeve in Wales. Suddenly he felt a tremendous longing for her, almost a hunger which made him feel ill. All he could think of was her sweet face, long blonde hair and the wide innocent eyes which could suddenly crinkle with amusement or flash with anger. He was tired of the city, of the filthy streets, the offal, the lay stalls thick with muck, the sluggish river, the arrogant courtiers, the bickering and in-fighting amongst the clerks and, above all, the animosity of the canons of St Paul: liars, lechers, men who should have been pursuing goodness but seemed to have lost their way. He felt impatient with the king who had put him to this task: a man intent on power, who honoured Corbett only because Corbett had served him well. Yet, all the clerk really wanted was to be in a lonely room in Neath Castle overlooking the wild seas, seated before a fire with Maeve in his arms. In his garret, Ranulf, busy congratulating himself on his rapid and lucky escape from the mercer's wife's bedroom, heard the faint lilting sound of the flute. He knew Corbett was sad and wished he could help. The playing went on into the early morning before it fell silent and only then did Ranulf know that his master had found some peace in sleep.

Corbett slept late the next morning, until he was abruptly woken by a pounding on the door below. Throwing a cloak round him, he hurried down and opened it. The mists outside swirled and boiled like steam from a cauldron. At first, he could see no-one.

'Who is there?' he called out and leapt back as a muddied figure, with a cut on his face, stepped into the house. At first the thought of a secret assassin crossed Corbett's mind but the man pulled back a rain-soaked hood and let the cloak fall from his shoulders.

'Master Corbett?'

'The same.'

'I am John Enderby, messenger from the Sheriff of Essex.' He handed a small scroll to Corbett, who instantly broke the red-and-white encrusted seal. The letter consisted of only four lines: the sheriff sent Corbett health and greetings; the information he had sent would be given to him by his messenger, John Enderby, the bearer of this letter.

Corbett crumpled the parchment in his hands. 'Please follow me.'

Enderby followed him up the stairs and, once Corbett had made him comfortable, the man delivered his message.

'The sheriff,' he said, 'was sorry he could not give a full written report but that would have taken more time. Suffice to say that the sheriff's men went to the manor of Cathall where they had found Walter de Montfort's steward, Thomas, dead; his throat had been cut. His wife Katherine had been raped a number of times by a notorious outlaw band, led by Robert Fitzwarren. They had apparently come to the manor to meet Thomas and, because of some quarrel, had cut his throat and raped the poor woman until she was half-crazed. The sheriff's men were able to calm Katherine, whereupon she confessed to the most extraordinary story. How the same outlaw Fitzwarren had raided convoys of travellers, traders and merchants on the roads leading out of London into Essex. Fitzwarren's plunder, however, was passed on to the Dean of St Paul's, who had sold it in the market-place of London and divided the money with the outlaw leader. On the day de Montfort died, his steward had been present in the congregation of St Paul's, having come to London to settle business on behalf of the outlaw. Because of his master's death, however, the steward was unable to conclude this business and returned empty-handed to the manor of Cathall. There, the outlaws, disappointed and frustrated, had taken out their rage on Thomas and his wife.'

'The Sheriff added,' Enderby wearily related, 'that although the woman was half crazed, a search of the house had revealed certain goods taken months earlier from a merchant. The sheriff sent his greetings and good wishes to His Grace and hoped the information would be of use.'

Corbett made Enderby repeat the story a number of times, satisfying himself on certain details before calling Ranulf down and instructing him to take Enderby to a nearby tavern to find him lodgings, before the messenger's return to Essex. Once he was gone, Corbett lay on the bed, his hands clasped behind his head, and once again considered de Montfort's death. So far, he had concentrated solely on the canons of St Paul's but there were others who would wish him dead. The courtesan had said this and she had also been present. Did Thomas, the steward, have a hand in this? Did he in fact kill his master? Was the king totally blameless? After all, and Corbett had consistently overlooked this fact, the king hated the de Montfort family. There were yet others who, if they had known de Montfort had been bought, would have gladly destroyed him. Was Robert Winchelsea, His Reverence the Archbishop of Canterbury, above murder? Corbett would have liked to think so but, having spent some time with the canons of St Paul's, believed priests and bishops were as capable of murder as any member of the laity. Finally, there were the barons. Corbett had heard rumours, about how the barons were gathering, plotting in secret meetings, trying to resist Edward's demands to follow him abroad.

Corbett let the questions swirl round his mind until he returned to the nagging half-memory of what he had seen on the altar. He had to concentrate on this matter, try and resolve it and perhaps some progress would be made. Accordingly, when Ranulf returned, Corbett asked him to go to St Paul's to seek out Sir Philip Plumpton and ask the canon, on the king's orders, to meet Corbett on the high altar once nones were completed. After that Corbett penned a short letter to the king describing what he had done and admitting that he had made little progress in the matter. He hoped the king would not be at Westminster when the message arrived. This would give him more time; for, if the king was displeased, he would simply send a curt order instructing Corbett to show some fruits of his hard labour.

The clerk spent the rest of the afternoon in his chamber

thinking over the details and the facts he had garnered about de Montfort's death. He became restless and would have gone out if it had not been for the cold mist seeping in through the chinks and cracks of the shutters. So he stayed inside, warming himself by the brazier. Corbett wrote a short message to Maeve, saying how much he missed her and hoped that spring would soon come so that he could see her again. He tried to joke about warming his heart and soul on the fires of her love and hoped it wouldn't read as clumsily as it sounded.

Ranulf returned and announced that he was going to the city. Corbett nodded absent-mindedly and let him go. Once his servant had clattered down the stairs, Corbett took up his flute, but only played a few notes before throwing it onto his bed. He opened the trunk at the bottom of his bed and took out a small leather pouch. Inside was Maeve's letter, now some four months old. The ivory-white vellum was beginning to turn slightly yellow but the handwriting was still as firm, curved and well formed as any scribe's. The halting phrases seemed to reflect the passion which existed between them.

> My dearest Hugh [it began],
>
> Affairs in Wales and around the castle of Neath are still not settled. My uncle says he is ill and has taken to his bed. He is as good an actor as any in a mummer's play. The countryside around is turning a golden yellow as summer fades and autumn begins. Strange that at such times of the year, partings from loved ones are all the more bitter. I miss you now more than ever. Every day, every waking moment, I think of your face, and would love to kiss your eyes and mouth. You must smile more, my serious clerk, the sun does rise and set without your leave. The shadows in your mind are nothing but dust on the leaf or wind through the trees. Yet I know you constantly live on the edge of darkness. Soon the night will be over, I shall be with you and the sun will always shine. I long for your touch. God keep you safe.
>
> Your lover, Maeve.

Corbett sighed as he rolled the letter up again and placed it in his pocket. Then he smiled, for he must have read the letter at least twice a day. He heard the wind howl outside and wished the iron-hard winter would break and Maeve would come. A knock on the door made him jump. He slid his hand under the bolster of the bed, his fingers touching the ice-cold handle of the dagger which lay there.

'Come in,' he snapped. The door swung open; Ranulf stood there, his hair wet, a bruise under his left eye. In his arms he held a bundle, cradling it clumsily like a bulky parcel.

'Come in!' Corbett repeated peevishly.

Ranulf, his face white with shock, his eyes glazed as if he had seen some terrible vision, walked slowly into the room like some sleep-walking dreamer. Wordlessly, he stretched out his hands, offering Corbett the bundle. The clerk took it apprehensively as the bundle stirred.

'It's a boy,' Ranulf murmured. 'A boy.'

Corbett pulled aside the edge of the tattered shawl and stared dumbstruck at what he saw, before bursting into peals of laughter and slumping on the bed. The baby, angry at being so rudely woken, flickered open his eyes and extended his mouth for one great bellow. The small pink face crumpled into a red mask and the tiny fists clenched on his chest, as the baby gave full vent to his fury. The cry seemed to shake Ranulf from his trance. He stood, arms dangling by his side, hopping from one foot to another, a look of abject horror on his face. Corbett controlled his laughter and gently cradled the baby in his arms. The infant, lips pursed, stopped his bawling and looked up speculatively at the clerk as if expecting some reward for its silence. Corbett rapped out a few instructions to Ranulf, who clattered downstairs to the buttery to bring back a bowl of warmed milk and a clean linen cloth. Corbett took the cloth and dipped it into the milk for the lusty infant to suck noisily.

'You are not,' the clerk began, 'to claim this is not yours,

Ranulf.' He looked down at the baby, the wisps of sandy hair, the small cleft chin, the dimple in the left cheek. If Corbett had found the baby in the street, he would have immediately recognized it as Ranulf's. Corbett made his servant pour two goblets of wine whilst the baby began positively to gnaw at the milk-soaked rag. After a few gulps of wine, the bemused father was calmer, more prepared to explain. He had gone out for a night's pleasure but, unfortunately, the father and elder brother of one of his earlier conquests had been waiting for him. A furious altercation ensued. Ranulf received a sharp blow to the face and his offspring was unceremoniously dumped into his arms. He gazed fearfully at his master.

'What, Master,' he muttered, 'are we going to do?' Corbett noted the word 'we' and glared at his servant. Some time soon, he really must have a quiet but very firm talk with this young man, who threatened to turn the house into a home for foundlings. The 'younger Ranulf', now angry at the cloth being drained of its milk, was beginning to look dangerously round the room trying to seek out the cause of his discomfort. Corbett hastily soaked the rag again and popped it into the infant's small extended mouth. 'Ranulf the younger' gripped it firmly and began to chew as vigorously as a young puppy.

The father, now beaming with smug pride at his young offspring, edged closer.

'What are we to do, Master Corbett?'

Corbett gently handed Ranulf his new-found son and, rising, went across to the trunk. He opened it, pulled out a clinking bag of coins and placed them gently into his servant's hands. He then took a writing tray and scribbled a hasty note, sealed it and handed it over to Ranulf.

'Look,' he said quietly, 'neither of us can care for this child. It has been baptized?'

Ranulf beamed and nodded.

'You,' Corbett continued wearily, 'are unable to look after yourself let alone an infant. God knows, you would probably lose the child the first time you took it out the door. You are to take this note to Adam Fenner, a cloth merchant in Candlewick Street. He and his wife have been longing for a child. They will look after this one, provide it with every necessity and positively spoil it with love and affection. They will let you see the child whenever you so wish.' He smiled sadly at Ranulf. 'Am I not right?'

Ranulf nodded, blinking vigorously to hide the tears welling up in his eyes. He scooped up the soft bundle.

'I am going to rename him Hugh,' he announced and quietly left the room.

Corbett heard his heavy footfalls on the stairs and silently despaired at Ranulf's innate penchant for mischief, shuddering to think that both father and son were now his responsibility. He then grinned at the thought for, once Maeve heard the news, she would shriek with laughter and tease Ranulf mercilessly.

Corbett wished he could look after the child, or return to his place at the Chancery, until Maeve arrived, and continue the work he did there every day, instead of walking in the sewer of human ambitions, greed, lechery and murder which surrounded de Montfort's death. Eventually, tired and weary, Corbett removed his boots and lay on his bed. He looked up into the darkness and waited for his servant to return, pretending to be asleep when Ranulf lifted the latch to his chamber and stealthily entered. His servant, taking a cloak from a bench, placed it carefully over his master and, extinguishing the candle, tiptoed out. Corbett smiled ruefully. He knew Ranulf and Ranulf knew him. His servant would know his master would never fall asleep with the candle lit but they both pretended. Corbett wondered how much more of his life would be pretence. Would it always go on like this? At last, his mind tired of whirling round, chasing shadows, dredging up memories, fell into an uneasy sleep.

The next morning Corbett, regretting his idleness of the previous day, rose and busied himself. Ranulf was roused and sent to Westminster with two letters: the first to the king; the second, Corbett hoped a royal messenger would deliver to Maeve, some time over the next few weeks. He instructed Ranulf to meet him at The Standard in Cheapside and, as his servant ran down the stairs, Corbett continued with his other tasks. There were provisions to be bought, matters to be dealt with. Finally, having dressed and armed himself, he wrapped a heavy, military cloak around him, went downstairs and out into Bread Street.

The city was still covered with a thick mist which made the figures he passed seem like phantasms from a dream. Underfoot, the ground was now slippery and ice-hard. Corbett stayed in the middle of the street and tried to avoid the hard-packed snow which was still falling off the roofs, whilst making every attempt not to slip into the sewer whch ran down the middle. Corbett soon found walking was now a very dangerous occupation. He stopped to help a fat-bottomed mercer's wife who had slipped onto her backside, a look of absolute amazement on her face. She would have sat there for the whole day, being taunted by urchins, had Corbett not come to help her. He strolled onto Cheapside and, turning right, entered the church of St Mary-le-Bow.

Corbett remembered the church when its doors and windows had been covered up with briars and the main gate barred. The whole place was excommunicated by the Archbishop of Canterbury, because it had been the headquarters of a satanic coven plotting against the king. Corbett recalled all this as he entered the church, fleetingly remembering Alice who had led the coven and with whom he had become deeply infatuated. He thought of her dark face and secretive eyes, realizing with a pang how the passage of years had still not really healed that wound. Now, however, St Mary's was different: clean, freshly painted, with new rectors installed and the school there recognized. It was now Corbett's parish church. In fact, he belonged to its fraternity of Corpus Christi, a society including aldermen, mercers, merchants and tradesmen, who had joined together for social and religious reasons. Corbett paid money every year for a chancery priest to sing masses for the repose of the souls of his wife and child and, though they did not know it, for the soul of Alice-atte-Bow, the leader of the satanic coven.

Corbett chatted to the priest, ensured all was well and became involved in a brief debate with one of the aldermen of the ward. London was divided into wards; it had twelve such, each with an alderman who supervized most of the secular and religious affairs in his quarter. Each person living there had to pay a tax. Corbett, although he could well afford it, had always resisted this because, by royal ordinance, clerks, together with knights and squires, were exempted from the levy. The alderman, however, was now insisting Corbett should pay for Ranulf; but the clerk evaded the issue claiming that because Ranulf was an apprentice-at-law he should also be excluded from this local tax. The alderman regretfully agreed. Corbett, however, failed to add that Ranulf's knowledge of the law was honoured more in the breach than in its observance. He also neglected to mention Ranulf's new addition to the ward.

13

As he moved from St Mary-le-Bow down Cheapside into Poultry, Corbett realized the city was at last trying to reassert itself against the inclement weather. The courts had certainly been busy. A line of felons and night-walkers, the whores in striped hoods and each carrying a white wand, were being led off to the prison at the Tun in Cornhill. The stocks were also full with bakers and fishmongers, their foul produce being burnt under their noses. Another man accused of slander had a whetstone round his neck and a placard calling him a false liar for all to ridicule.

As Corbett saw the whores he remembered Abigail, the woman who lived in de Montfort's house in Candlewick Street. Again he wondered if she had played a part in the murder. She had been present at the mass and de Montfort, never the most pleasant of people, had threatened her with public insult; any whore thrice convicted could be whipped from prison to the city bounds and told to abjure the city for ever. There again, and so Corbett dismissed the idea, if de Montfort's liaison with any courtesan was known, he too would be taken to the open prison at the Tun at Cornhill and there exposed all day for public ridicule. Corbett stopped to watch the chaos surrounding a huge canopied wagon which had overturned, spilling its produce out into the slushy show. The carter and his apprentices were driving off the urchins and would-be thieves. The confusion he was watching reflected what was going on in his own mind. Why should a man who had achieved so much risk it all in order to manage a brothel? De Montfort would have fallen from grace if that had become public knowledge. Perhaps the solution was to do with frustrated arrogance: de Montfort, having reached the pinnacle of his career, perhaps believed he could do things forbidden to others and specifically denied to priests?

Corbett found Ranulf waiting for him and gave him some silver to go and purchase certain foodstuffs they needed; whilst he went to the shop of his banker, Gisors the goldsmith, a modest affair which seemed to argue against the accumulated wealth of the merchant. Inside, Corbett looked around at the neatly stacked leather trunks and the parchment rolls, each docketed and tagged, listing those who had banked with Gisors, to whom he had lent gold and at what rates. In spite of the Church's ruling about usury, the banking and depositing of money was now a thriving business in the capital. The goldsmith greeted Corbett with his usual subservience. The clerk was a regular and trusted customer, the sort, beloved by any banker, who deposits silver and gold and rarely takes away again. This morning, however, Corbett disappointed him. Usually, the clerk stayed and shared the gossip of the court and the palace, information, however petty, Gisors could always use. This morning the clerk was curt, absent-minded; he stated what he wanted and, once Gisors had counted the money out into a small leather purse, took it with a mutter of thanks and left the shop.

Corbett breakfasted in the tavern where he was joined by Ranulf, who had spent a profitable hour buying the provisions they needed. He returned the little that was left of Corbett's silver.

The clerk looked down at it. 'Is that all?'

'Yes, Master.'

Corbett groaned quietly. He had been so engrossed in this matter and other affairs of the court that he had neglected to keep an eye on his money. He had forgotten how the cruel winter would have sent the price of goods soaring. Two loaves usually cost a penny, but now the price had doubled; the same went for vegetables, meat, drink and anything brought into the city from the country. Once Ranulf had eaten, they left and went back up Cheapside towards St Paul's. The mist was beginning to lift and there were more people in the market-place. So immersed was Corbett in the coming meeting with Plumpton, giving half an ear to Ranulf's protests about the price of things, that neither he nor his servant noticed the young man with slit eyes, pock-marked face and long greasy hair, dressed completely in black, who had followed them from the tavern like a bird of evil omen. The fellow kept them under scrutiny until they entered the precincts of St Paul's, then he smiled and, with a nod of satisfaction, walked away.

In the courtyard Corbett stopped so Ranulf could watch the end of a miracle play. The stage was set on a two-storied affair on wheels, the lower tier where the actors dressed, the upper for the play itself. The stage, and its brilliant backdrop of a grotesquely painted mouth of hell with demons leaping out of it, was topped by a roof and a huge silver griffin. The story was of the Passion. The actor playing Christ, costumed in a white robe and a silver-braided wig, drew the sympathetic murmurs of the surrounding crowd; while Pilate, in his purple cloak and false red hair, drew jeers, boos, catcalls and the occasional piece of dirt. Ranulf would have stayed there longer but Corbett, tiring of the scene and fearful of the pickpockets he had recognized entering the crowd (one of them from a court case he'd attended a few months previously), pulled his protesting servant up into the doorway of the cathedral. The nave was crowded and noisy with business: parchment-sellers, professional scribes, lawyers talking loudly, servants waiting to be hired. They pushed through these and made their way up into the choir; by the smell of candle-grease and incense, Corbett knew that nones had just finished.

They found Plumpton in the sacristy. The priest looked surly and exclaimed in anger at Corbett's request,

'What do you mean, man? That I lay out the entire altar as it was.' The priest looked as if he was about to refuse. 'Again,' Corbett wearily added, 'I must remind you that I do not do this out of any sense of power or pleasure. I am simply following His Grace's request. I would be grateful, Sir Philip, if you would see it done, now.'

Corbett went out and sat in the sanctuary chair whilst Plumpton, aided by a number of servants, pulled back the green gold-embroidered covering cloth and laid the altar as it was after mass.

'Sir Philip,' Corbett called out, 'I would not like it arranged as if mass was beginning, but as you remember it when you cleared the altar after it was finished.'

Sir Philip glared at him and nodded. It took some time, but Plumpton, now warming to his task, brought on the cruet dish which held the water and wine, two long, glass-stemmed jugs with a cluster of golden grapes on the caps, each set in a pure silver dish. He laid out the white linen cloths the priests used to clean the chalice and their fingers; even a few unconsecrated hosts were scattered about.

Once he pronounced himself satisfied, Corbett went up and inspected the altar. He ordered the candles to be lit to give the right reflection, positioning himself where de Montfort would have stood and where he himself had been when examining the altar on behalf of the king. De Montfort's chalice was there, the wine winking in the light, the cruets to the far side, one containing the water three-quarters filled, the wine cruet completely empty.

'You have forgotten to put wine in this?' Corbett asked.

Plumpton shook his head. 'No, it was empty after the mass. I remember, because there was no wine to throw away.'

Corbett nodded. There was something missing, something he had not grasped. He could feel his stomach churning with excitement. He looked again, putting the altar scene firmly in his mind. He imagined he was staring at a picture, some stained-glass window he found impressive or beautiful and always wanted to remember.

'Sir Philip,' he said eventually, 'I thank you. I cannot find the solution. Perhaps you may.' He then turned on his heel and walked out of St Paul's.

It was early afternoon, the mist had not lifted during the day and was now thickening as evening drew in. The play in the cathedral courtyard had finished and in Cheapside the markets were closing early, the merchants setting the obligatory lantern-horns outside their houses. Only the beggars and scavengers, those looking to cull what they could from a day's trading, were there. A group of horsemen rode by, the hooves of their mounts breaking and scattering the ice. Corbett nearly slipped and suddenly realized Ranulf was missing. He had been with him when he went into the cathedral but, as was customary, he had once again slipped away to his own private pleasures. Corbett shrugged. He felt hungry and bought a pie from a baker but, after two bites, tossed it away, for he could taste the rancid meat beneath the spices. He went into the tavern on the corner of Bread Street and sat near the fire warming himself with a bowl of soup. He tried to ignore the globules of fat bobbing about amongst the pieces of meat and vegetable by drinking three tankards of London ale, specially spiced and warmed to keep off the chill. Afterwards, he went outside, relieved himself in the gutter and, turning the corner, made his way down to his lodgings.

Corbett was used to violence; he had fought in Scotland and Wales and been the victim of ambush but the attack that evening was as sudden and savage as he had ever experienced. He was gingerly trying to avoid the open sewer, at the same time keeping his feet on the ice, when a figure in black stepped out of a doorway. If Corbett hadn't seen the glint of steel, the sword would have taken his head off in one chopping curve. Corbett instead swerved and sprang away. He slipped on the ice and fell, squirming as his assailant, his eyes glaring through holes in the black hood, brought his sword up for a crashing blow. Corbett, his legs caught in his cloak, his sword slewed round making it impossible for him to draw, scurried backwards like a child facing an irate parent. He felt his hand slip into the sewer, as the assassin-cum-executioner, still advancing, held up the sword and searched where to give the death blow. Corbett could not even think of what to do. He sat transfixed, watching those dreadful eyes and the curve of the sword behind the man's shoulder. He knew this was no alley bully or common felon but an assassin; the man was calm, rhythmic in his movements, like a dancer taking his time. And why not? The streets were empty, it was dusk and who would care that a man stupid enough to go out on his own was now being attacked? Corbett tried to call for help but his mouth was dry and the sound stuck like a piece of unchewed food in his throat. He found the dagger in his belt and pulled it out, but that only made him slip further on the icy ground. He looked up in desperation as the man, legs now apart, prepared to bring the sword down for the killing blow. The assassin came forward. Suddenly, he threw his head back and, crumpling like a loose piece of cloth, slumped onto his knees, his sword slipping out of his hand, his head falling forward onto his chest. Corbett saw the blood dribble out of his mouth. The assassin coughed and, gently toppling over to one side, curled up like a child going to sleep. Corbett looked up. Ranulf stood there, grinning broadly, feet apart, in his hand a long dagger bloodied right up to the hilt.

'For God's sake, man,' Corbett said testily, 'I never heard you arrive!'

Ranulf shrugged and squatted down to wipe the dagger on the dead assassin's cloak.

'I'll never understand, Master Corbett,' he said drily, 'when I'm around, you hardly talk to me. When I am here you have only criticisms. Do you wish I had come later?'

'Where have you been? It was a miracle that you did come.' Corbett spoke snappily with fright.

'I was outside the cathedral,' Ranulf said, his voice rising in protest. 'I went to watch the stage, I saw you disappear round the corner and I followed. I was going to catch you up but I saw this character.' Ranulf nudged the dead body with his foot. 'He seemed to appear from nowhere. He followed you so I decided to stay back to see what would happen. The rest you know.'

Corbett smiled.

'I am grateful, Ranulf. I am sorry I was angry with you.'

Ranulf, however, refused to be mollified. 'I waited. Once his back was turned it was easy. He never,' he added with pride, 'heard me. Neither did you. Did you?'

Corbett grinned. 'No, I did not, Ranulf. But I have never been so pleased to see you. Here, help me up.'

Ranulf helped the clerk back to his feet, solicitously dusting the back of his cloak off, smacking hard as if relishing every brush with his hand.

'Thank you, Ranulf. That will do.'

Corbett squatted down again beside the assassin, turned him over on his back and pulled off the hood. He had never seen the man before, the staring eyes, the thin sallow face, the greasy hair, the pock-marked skin. A professional assassin. London was full of them, ex-soldiers, veterans from the wars, men prepared to carry out a murder for a bag of silver.

Corbett rose. 'I'll be fine now, Ranulf. It's best if you go and see the alderman. Tell him what happened. Tell him if he has any questions to direct them to the king, but ask him to send men for the body.'

Ranulf needed no second bidding. Any opportunity to lecture the portly, pompous alderman, whose young wife

Ranulf had long lusted after, could not be resisted. In spite of the slippery ice, he ran down Bread Street and back into Cheapside. The sooner the task was done, the sooner he could visit his son.

Corbett climbed back to his chamber and poured himself a generous cupful of wine. He sat on the edge of his bed holding the goblet between his hands, now and again taking deep draughts as he tried to control the trembling in his body and calm his churning stomach. He felt he might disgrace himself and vomit due to a mixture of fear and relief at his unexpected deliverance from death. The darkness drew in and Corbett, now fearful of the night, lit the candles. He refilled the goblet and collected his thoughts; the assassin had been sent by someone, undoubtedly one of the priests of St Paul's. Corbett realized he must be close to the solution of the mystery, or else the assassin would never have been sent. Once again he wondered what he had learnt but had so far misunderstood. He looked down at the goblet and swirled the wine around absent-mindedly. Suddenly, like an arrow speeding out of the darkness, Corbett knew what he had missed. He became so excited he refilled his cup, took five or six deep draughts and swirled the lees of the drink around the cup before replenishing it again. He now remembered what he had seen on the high altar the day de Montfort had died and, at the same time, remembered the stain on the cope in the cupboard in the sacristy. He would have liked to have returned to St Paul's but realized that the people he wanted to question had probably left. Moreover, the rapid gulps of wine were making their presence felt. He was tired, sleepy, so he extinguished the candle, bolted the door and sat in the darkness trying to calm the excited beating of his heart.

In St Paul's Sir Philip Plumpton was likewise excited. It had first begun while singing vespers in the choir. He had intoned the responsorial verses along with the other canons, letting his mind drift back to the events earlier in the day. He gazed up into the sanctuary, recalling how he had laid out the chalice, patens, monstrances, cruets and candles for Corbett. He remembered every item and how the altar had looked after de Montfort's death. – That was his job and Sir Philip was proud of how carefully he had replicated matters for that sanctimonious clerk. Even minor details like the cruets. Sir Philip stopped his mindless chanting. No, he had forgotten something. He gasped in surprise. 'No,' he murmured to himself. 'It had been the same as on the morning de Montfort had died but it shouldn't have been. Oh, no!'

Sir Philip's excitement was such that he dropped the book from which he was chanting the responses and, gazing around apologetically, stooped down to pick it up. He continued the divine service but with his mind on the murderer's flawed plan. Had Corbett realized it? And if he told the clerk what would happen?

During the meal in the refectory of the chapter-house Sir Philip's excitement grew so much that he could hardly eat. He was nervous, agitated, refusing food but drinking deeply, so he drew the curious glances of his colleagues though he would not be drawn. He could hardly wait to gabble through compline, not bothering, as was his wont, to stay in the cathedral to pray and reflect on the day's events. Sir Philip was not a bad man but one always in a hurry and that night more than most. Alone in the chamber, still obsessed with his discovery, he heard a knock on the door.

'Come in,' he called and turned back to his desk, pen in hand as he prepared to write his thoughts down on a piece of parchment. If Sir Philip had turned, perhaps he would have lived. However, so immersed was he in his own thoughts that he let the visitor into his chamber – allowing Death to wrap the cord round his neck, pull it tight and, after a few gasping, throttling seconds, Sir Philip's life was extinguished as quickly and as effortlessly as the murderer licked his fingers and doused the candles in the chamber.

14

Corbett was up early the next morning, the fears, anxieties and tremblings of the previous evening quite gone. The wine had soothed his nerves and Corbett was intent on resolving the mystery of de Montfort's death once and for all. It had hung around his neck like a whetstone and he was angry at how his blindness had kept him caught like some criminal in the stocks. He roused Ranulf and questioned the sleepy servant on what he had done the previous evening, satisfying himself that the ward's watch had been notified of the assassin's death and the body taken away. Corbett then roughly instructed Ranulf to follow him to St Paul's and, ignoring his servant's grumbles and muttered protests about the base ingratitude of certain masters, especially high-ranking clerks from the Chancery, bundled him out of the door. Ranulf protested meekly at the lack of breakfast so they stopped at a baker's stall and bought a fresh, hot loaf, which Corbett thrust into Ranulf's hands, telling him to eat as they walked along.

The morning mist was beginning to lift and a faint sun was already making its presence felt when they entered the deserted courtyard of St Paul's. They found the cathedral locked, but the chapter-house was in uproar.

The Scotsman, Ettrick, solemnly informed them of what had happened. The canons had risen at dawn to sing divine office and heard the terrible news that Sir Philip Plumpton had been brutally murdered, the wire of the garrotte still round his throat. Corbett closed his eyes and murmured a quiet requiem for the fat, rather silly priest's soul, now going to meet its maker. Corbett allowed the Scotsman to take him up to the dead priest's chamber on the second storey of the chapter-house. Corbett gave Plumpton's poor corpse a cursory examination: the priest's eyes were still wide open, little attempt having been made to remove the horror and shock of death. Corbett crossed himself and, turning, asked Ettrick if he could question certain servants. He brushed aside the Scotsman's protests, insisting such an interrogation was essential and should be done immediately. The clerk secretly hoped he was not talking to the murderer but, even if he was, this might only hasten matters and perhaps help flush the assassin out into the open.

The servants named were brought to him and ruthlessly questioned; Corbett took them back to the days after de Montfort's death. Who had approached them? Who had assigned their duties? When he had satisfied himself, Corbett told them to leave the cathedral and not to return for at least four days. He gave the two servants in question three silver coins, to buy their silence and arrange their swift departure from the cathedral precincts. After which, Corbett, with Ranulf in tow, quietly left St Paul's for a nearby tavern. Corbett, armed with sword, dagger and a mail shirt hidden beneath his tunic, was confident that de Montfort's murderer would not try an assassination attempt so soon after the failure of the first. Provided he stayed with the crowd and away from solitary places, Corbett felt safe. In the tavern he surprised Ranulf with his generosity, ordering the best ale and food the place could serve. Once his servant had eaten Corbett asked him to find a young friend, an acquaintance and bring him to the tavern as soon as possible. The servant looked at his strange master and was about to protest, but one look at Corbett's stern face and hard eyes convinced him it would be useless.

The clerk had to wait for at least two hours before

Ranulf returned. The young man he brought was personable enough for Corbett's uses. The fellow introduced himself as Richard Tallis but Corbett, brushing aside his friendly greetings, entrusted him with a message: he was to go to the Cathedral of St Paul's and seek out a certain priest Corbett named and ask if that priest would be kind enough, before vespers, to hear the confession of someone who believed he had committed a terrible sin and wanted to confess it to him alone. Tallis looked surprised and Corbett thought he was about to protest but, after two gold coins had exchanged hands, Richard promised he would do his utmost and, unless Corbett heard to the contrary, everything would happen as arranged.

For the rest of the afternoon Corbett stayed in the tavern replenishing his drink as he carefully went over what he had learnt in the last few days. Corbett believed he had found the murderer of de Montfort, the would-be regicide, the slayer of Plumpton and the man who had attempted to kill him by proxy the previous evening. Corbett felt as satisfied as he ever would in this world that he had uncovered the truth, but believed it would be futile to confront the culprit with his evidence. Better to allow the man to confess his own guilt and thus meet his just rewards.

The hours seemed to drag but at last Corbett gauged the time had come for him to return to St Paul's. Ranulf, who had spent the afternoon wandering in and out of the tavern on a number of minor errands, was asked to go with him. His servant, of course, agreed willingly, for he sensed that his master was close to the kill. Ranulf knew Corbett, with his own devious sly ways, was about to bring a murderer to justice and he, who hated the fat priests and their grasping hypocritical ways, fully intended to see matters reach their climax. Corbett, however, insisted that although Ranulf was to accompany him into the cathedral, he was to stay in the background.

St Paul's was empty when they entered. Because of

winter, business finished early in the afternoon and the place was so cold that few people bothered to linger longer than necessary. Corbett went up to the confessional, the place where the priest would sit and shrive the sins of those seeking repentance. It was really a wooden trellis screen attached to a pillar. The priest sat on one side with his back to it, while the penitent would knee on a small wooden stool on the other. Corbett knelt and waited. He heard a sound from far beyond the sanctuary, a door opening and closing and the soft slithering sound of a man walking towards the screen. The priest sat down murmuring the '*In nomine Patris*' followed by the '*benedicte*' and quietly invited Corbett to begin his confession. The clerk, in a whisper to disguise his voice, began with the usual ritual.

'Forgive me, Father, for I have sinned.' Corbett stated the last time he had been shriven and mentioned a number of sins, those which immediately sprung to mind and, even though he was in danger, Corbett smiled wryly as he realized that most of his offences were either lustful thoughts or anger towards Ranulf. He heard the priest stir angrily at being called out to absolve such minor offences. So Corbett, steeling himself, his hands now dropping to the hilt of his dagger, began the most dreadful confession he had ever made.

'Father, I know a murderer, the name of the man,' he continued hurriedly, 'who has killed two men, plotted to murder the king, the Lord's anointed, and has tried to murder someone else.' The priest stirred but Corbett continued remorselessly. 'Father, what am I to do? In justice, should I keep this information to myself? Or should I hand it over to the authorities?'

The priest turned towards the screen.

'No, Master Corbett,' Robert de Luce hissed through the screen. 'You have come to the right place.'

In the faint light of the cathedral, Corbett stared through the holes of the lattice screen at de Luce's hard, angry eyes. He sensed the man was mad, not witless like some fool in the streets, but a man driven to insanity by hate. The look of malice in de Luce's eyes was something tangible. Corbett felt sudden dread, and wondered whether this dramatic confrontation of the murderer was the wisest possible course of action.

'I have come,' Corbett said, dropping all pretence, 'to tell you what I know. To ask you to confess to what is true. You, Robert de Luce, treasurer of the Cathedral of St Paul's, the senior canon in this church, murdered Walter de Montfort during the sacrifice of the mass, attempted to murder me because I was near the truth and certainly killed Philip Plumpton because he too discovered it. I also believe deep in my heart, though I cannot prove this, that you intended to murder His Grace the King: the poisoned chalice was meant for him.'

'And how do you know all this, my clever clerk?' de Luce rasped.

'The chalice,' Corbett replied, 'first went to those on the Dean's right, de Eveden and Ettrick, before being passed on de Montfort's left to Plumpton, yourself and Blaskett. You knew de Eveden only pretended to drink the wine so enough would be left to disguise the poison you sprinkled as you grasped the chalice after Blaskett had drunk. And who would glimpse this sleight of hand? Your colleagues had just taken the sacrament and would stand heads bowed, eyes closed. Logic dictates either you or Plumpton was the poisoner. Plumpton's dead so it has to be you. You forgot one thing: the *Hostiam pacis* – the kiss of peace. De Montfort had to offer the chalice to the king and, before doing so, drink from it again. This is where your plot to slay the king went wrong. De Montfort drank the poisoned chalice and immediately fell dead. In the confusion you took de Montfort's chalice and, under your chasuble, dashed the lees of the poisoned wine onto your own garments. It wouldn't be much. After all, five men had drunk from it – de Montfort twice. The chalice bowl was small, it would contain little wine. Yet when I went up to the altar, after de

Montfort's death, I found the chalice almost full. I suggest, Sir Priest, that after you dashed the chalice against your cope, you seized a cruet and refilled the chalice with wine. Actually, you needed only to put in a few drops, but, of course, you filled it too full. Yesterday Sir Philip Plumpton realized that the chalice was full when it should have been empty, and, secondly, that there was no wine left in the cruet. Of course there wasn't – you had poured what was left into de Montfort's chalice!'

De Luce sniggered. 'Very clever. But surely there would have been a trace of poison in the chalice?'

'Oh, yes, but you made sure it was gone. Beneath your chasuble, in the confusion following de Montfort's death, you wiped the chalice completely clean. Only it left a stain on both the chasuble and alb. I saw them when I met you and the other canons in the sacristy. After Sir Philip's death it was simply a matter of interrogating the two laundresses who work here. They told me that in the afternoon of the same day de Montfort died, you gave them an alb to clean, giving them strict instructions to remove all stains. The chasuble you ignored: it is too heavy to clean, such stains were commonplace and no one could really prove they had been acquired when you wore it at that fatal mass. The alb was different. Isn't it strange, priest, that in your arrogance, you never thought of washing it yourself? Mind you,' Corbett continued, 'there were other signs. The drops of poisoned wine on the altar frontal. They were still there after you dashed the wine under your chasuble. Finally, the wine on the carpet, to the left of where de Montfort had stood. In your haste to refill the chalice after de Montfort's death, some wine had fallen on the ground. It must have been spilt then. You know Canon Law, and de Montfort was a rigid disciplinarian. If consecrated wine had been spilt during mass there would have been an elaborate ritual to clean it up afterwards.'

'Is that all, Clerk?' de Luce hissed.

'Oh, no,' Corbett replied. 'You hoped that once de

Montfort was dead, the dean's scandalous private life would cloud the identity of his murderer. You even tried to pass the blame on to other people. De Montfort, ever the boastful man, had declared that the king had sent him a pannikin of wine. Once you had refilled the chalice, and while de Montfort's body was being taken to the sacristy for anointment by Blaskett, it was simply a matter of slipping up to de Montfort's room, poisoning the wine and, under your heavy ceremonial cope, bringing it down to the small vestry in the sacristy. I am right, am I not, Sir Priest?'

'Oh, you are, Clerk,' de Luce replied, his eyes glittering with malice behind the screen.

'Only one problem remains, de Luce,' Corbett snapped – 'why?'

De Luce cocked his head to one side as if this was a real problem. 'Oh, it is quite easy,' he said in a sing-song whisper. 'You see, I did not intend de Montfort to die, though I did not mourn his death, but our beloved king was a different matter. You see, Corbett, have you ever lost someone you loved? I did. I had a brother. I loved him more than any other person in the world. I do not know if you have studied my background, Corbett. Perhaps you will and will find I was born in Flanders. I came here and was promoted in the English king's service. Edward himself offered me the benefice here and, in doing so, I extended the royal favour to my own brother. A merchant, he came over to England, expanded his business and, because of Edward's involvement in Scotland, went to Berwick. He was there, in the Red House, when Edward put it to the sack as if he was some new Attila or Genghis Khan. My brother died, so did his pleasant-faced, innocent wife,' de Luce's voice cracked under the strain, '... their lovely children. You see, Corbett, the king had to pay for these murders. No one gave him the right to sack cities. No one gave him the right to slay an innocent man, a beloved brother, his wife and young children just because the burgesses of Berwick were stupid enough to hold out longer than they should have done. When I heard the news I resolved that Edward should die. Not quietly. But in the open. In the sight of the Church, of Edward's parliament, and in the eyes of God, if there is one. Edward would fall dead and my brother's death would be avenged.' De Luce picked at the screen absent-mindedly with his finger, a half smile on his lips, a faraway look in his eyes. Corbett felt afraid. The man was completely mad but hid it under a mask of cold reasonableness.

'You see, Corbett, I had forgotten that de Montfort would drink from the chalice again. If that fool Ettrick had not reminded him, my plan would have worked and de Montfort would have been blamed. Men would have seen it as proof that the de Montfort family had not forgotten their persecution at the hands of King Edward. But,' he shrugged as if it was a matter of little importance, 'de Montfort did drink it again and my plan was thwarted. But then I saw further possibilities. If I wanted men to believe that de Montfort had killed the king, why should not the king kill de Montfort during the sacrifice of the mass? The scandal, the blasphemy, the sacrilege, would weaken Edward in the eyes of everyone in Western Christendom, not only in England.'

Corbett watched de Luce intently and saw the madness in the priest's eyes.

'You are right,' the priest continued smoothly. 'Everything was confusion after de Montfort collapsed. It was simply a matter of going to the altar, as if to arrange certain items, and pick the chalice up. I lifted my chasuble and dashed what was left of the wine against my alb, rubbing it clean before refilling it. Nobody would notice and, if they did, I would have some satisfactory explanation. I thought it would work until your interfering questions began but, even then, I thought I was safe. After all no one loved de Montfort. His whore had been present at mass. Blaskett and de Eveden feared him, Plumpton envied him and, of course, dear Ettrick, the Scotsman, he was the one who reminded de Montfort to drink the wine a second time.' De Luce now looked directly at Corbett. 'And you, with your meddling ways! And your half-finished questions. By all rights you know,' de Luce continued conversationally, 'you should be dead now. I knew Plumpton had deduced something. The fat fool's excitement last night convinced me that the farce you made him go through yesterday morning had awakened his usually dormant brain and fitful memory. So I killed him.'

De Luce smiled. His hands dropped down. 'And now, Corbett, your penance!'

Hugh would always regret he had not watched this mad, evil priest more intently. Only when the word 'penance' was uttered did he begin to move away, but it was too late. De Luce, the smile still on his twisted lips, managed to thrust the long, thin, stiletto-like dagger through a small aperture deep into Corbett's shoulder. The clerk screamed at the red-hot pain, his hand going up to feel the blood pumping out and collapsing as de Luce moved quickly out of the screen and up the cathedral. He heard voices, Ranulf shouting, the sound of drawn swords and the whirr of a crossbow bolt. Then the darkness mercifully obliterated his agony.

Corbett woke a few days later in a lime-washed chamber of St Bartholomew's Hospital. The mattress was soft enough, slung over a low truckle bed. He glanced round and saw the black crucifix on the wall, a bench, two stools and a small table. He knew he was in St Bartholomew's because Father Thomas was standing there, his back to him, mixing some potion at the table. Corbett stirred and called out.

Father Thomas turned round, his face beaming with pleasure. 'So, Hugh, you have decided to rejoin us.'

Corbett struggled to rise, but a hot knifing pain, which shot from his shoulder all the way down his right side, forced him back on the bed. He could feel the sweat pouring down his face and body.

'You should lie still, Hugh,' Father Thomas said, a note of authority in his usually gentle voice. He bathed the clerk's head with a cloth dipped in warm, herb-strewn water and, bringing a small cup, held Corbett's head and forced the clerk to drink the dark, bitter mixture.

'This will make you sleep eventually,' the monk said.

Hugh lay back and stared up at the ceiling. 'How long have I been here?' he asked.

'Eight days.'

'What happened?'

Father Thomas patted Hugh on the head as if he was a child.

'Stay there.'

He went to the door and called down the passageway. Ranulf came in wringing his hands, his face a picture of concern and compassion. Behind him was Maeve. Corbett could hardly believe his eyes and, if he had not been warned by the pain, he would have sprung out of bed. She came quietly into the room, pulled a stool over and sat down beside him. Taking one of his hands in hers, she kissed it gently and stroked it affectionately, just looking at him. Corbett realized how beautiful she was, the bright corn-coloured hair peeping out beneath the dark blue wimple over her head. Her face, however, was paler than usual, almost alabaster, and her eyes larger and darker. He could see the dark shadows of sleeplessness around them.

'Maeve, when did you arrive?' he said huskily. 'I thought you were in Wales. The roads? How could you get through?'

Maeve smiled. 'We did not come by road but by sea.'

Corbett clasped her hand tightly until she winced. 'It is so good to see you.'

Ranulf, the clerk's servant, had been standing there, his look of concern now replaced by one of deep grievance at being ignored.

'Ranulf, what happened at St Paul's?'

Ranulf shrugged. 'I heard you yell. I saw the priest leave and come from behind the screen, the dagger still in his hand. I had brought a crossbow, and even in that light he was still a good enough target.'

'You killed him?'

Ranulf shrugged again and smiled. 'Of course. The bolt went straight into the back of his neck. He died very quickly before the high altar, just near the anker house.' Ranulf went over and sat on a bench against the far wall. 'He cursed you before he died, while the anchorite behind his wall shouted out about how God's justice had visited his temple and that the evil man would go down into the deep pit of hell, and so on, and so on.'

'And the king?'

Ranulf gave a sigh. 'He sends his thanks. I told Hervey what had happened. He wrote some of it down and gave it to the king.'

Corbett groaned. The one thing he did not want was someone reporting back, putting words in his mouth.

'Did the king seem pleased?'

'Very. As I said, he thanked you.' Ranulf thought that now was not the time to tell about the heavy clinking purse the king had tossed to him.

'Does he want to see me?'

Ranulf shook his head. 'Oh, no. He said you were to rest. He's off to Flanders, taking an army there. But he said he would see you on his return.'

Corbett nodded and again thought of his favourite verse from the psalms: 'Put not your trust in Princes.' The king was as fickle as the sun in winter. He thought back to St Paul's, again seeing de Luce's eyes glaring at him through the screen, and cursed his own stupidity and folly. He should have been more cautious. Yet Maeve had come. The only woman, indeed, the only person, he had ever really loved.

'And how long will you be here?'

'Oh, for months,' she said. 'Long enough for you to get better and for us to get married.'

Corbett could have shouted with joy. He felt the winter outside had broken, the spring had come at last and there was something to live for.

Conclusion

This novel is based on fact. Edward I brutally sacked Berwick and burned the Red House of the Flemings because they refused to surrender. Edward did hold a great assembly of the realm at St Paul's, at which Walter de Montfort had been appointed to argue vehemently against the king's right to tax the Church. His death took place as described, violently and suddenly, leaving men wondering whether God was punishing Edward of England or vindicating royal rights. The Church did eventually reach a compromise with Edward as did his barons. The king waged a successful war in Flanders, but in Scotland the sack of Berwick proved to be a point of no return and the Scots refused to submit.